ALLEN COUNTY PUBLIC LIBRARY
S0-BWS-996

SPECIAL MESSAGE TO READERS

This book is published by

THE ULVERSCROFT FOUNDATION,

a registered charity in the U.K., No. 264873

The Foundation was established in 1974 to provide funds to help towards research, diagnosis and treatment of eye diseases. Below are a few examples of contributions made by THE ULVERSCROFT FOUNDATION:

★ A new Children's Assessment Unit at Moorfield's Hospital, London.

★ Twin operating theatres at the Western Ophthalmic Hospital, London.

★ The Frederick Thorpe Ulverscroft Chair of Ophthalmology at the University of Leicester.

★ Eye Laser equipment to various eye hospitals.

If you would like to help further the work of the Foundation by making a donation or leaving a legacy, every contribution, no matter how small, is received with gratitude. Please write for details to:

THE ULVERSCROFT FOUNDATION,
The Green, Bradgate Road, Anstey,
Leicestershire, LE7 7FU. England.

Telephone: (0533) 364325

Love is
a time of enchantment:
in it all days are fair and all fields
green. Youth is blest by it,
old age made benign: the eyes of love see
roses blooming in December,
and sunshine through rain. Verily
is the time of true-love
a time of enchantment—and
Oh! how eager is woman
to be bewitched!

CORRIGAN'S ISLAND

Matthew Corrigan has returned to Inveree after an absence of many years, and there is no trace of the boy Morwenna knew in the stranger he has become. Can she believe the reasons he gives for his return—or are more sinister motives the truth behind the matter? What is the truth about his relationship with April and why is Morwenna's father so disturbed when he learns of Matthew's presence on the island?

For My Father

MARIAN HIPWELL

CORRIGAN'S ISLAND

Complete and Unabridged

ULVERSCROFT
Leicester

First published in Great Britain in 1988 by
Robert Hale Ltd.,
London

First Large Print Edition
published January 1991
by arrangement with
Robert Hale Ltd.,
London

British Library CIP Data

Hipwell, Marian
Corrigan's Island.—Large print ed.—
Ulverscroft large print series: romance
I. Title
823.914[F]

ISBN 0-7089-2349-6

Published by
F. A. Thorpe (Publishing) Ltd.
Anstey, Leicestershire

Set by Rowland Phototypesetting Ltd.
Bury St. Edmunds, Suffolk
Printed and bound in Great Britain by
T. J. Press (Padstow) Ltd., Padstow, Cornwall

1

IT was a misty day in late summer when Matthew Corrigan fulfilled his promise to return to Inveree.

Hunched over the accounts at the reception desk of the Beachcomber Guest House, Morwenna did not immediately look up as he entered and closed the door behind him. Then he spoke and she recognised his voice instantly, even though it was years since she had heard it.

"Morwenna!" He was staring at her, momentarily caught off his guard. "I didn't expect—that is, I thought you'd left—"

"I've been back some time now." Recovering from her own surprise with an effort, she smiled at him. "Hello, Matthew."

His eyebrows arched.

"You remember me then, after all this time?"

Disconcerted, Morwenna looked away from him. How could she have forgotten him? Matthew Corrigan, the playmate and confidant of herself and her brother, Phil; the rich man's son with whom they had shared so many carefree summers, darting among the coves and beaches with which the coast abounded, Matthew himself growing so tanned and unkempt in the process he was soon indistinguishable from the island children. Yet a boy whose expensive clothes and refined ways she had so mistrusted at first, she recalled now. She caught his thoughtful gaze, the dark, almost brooding, eyes which seemed to be measuring her, as if he, too, looked for some semblance of the girl he'd known so long ago. Aware that he was awaiting her reply, Morwenna shrugged.

"You were a part of the scene for so long, until you stopped coming," she murmured.

"I told you I'd come back," he said.

Morwenna eyed him silently. He hadn't told her it would take him over ten years to fulfil that promise . . . Ten years in which the reserved boy had, judging by first impressions, grown into an equally serious man. How old would he be now? He'd been nearer Phil's age than hers; she had been the young nuisance of a sister who had trailed after them, insisting on being included in their activities, resentful of their close friendship and the way the newcomer from the mainland had seemingly replaced her in her cherished older brother's affections.

Almost as if reading her thoughts, Matthew's eyes twinkled suddenly.

"You're all 'growed up', Morwenna!" he remarked.

Aware of his frankly approving gaze, she coloured. This was not what she remembered. They had been equals, comrades in summer escapades, even though he'd begun to occupy more and more of her thoughts in that last summer, made even more poignant in her memory because she had not known it would be the last. A leggy ten year old, she had begun to look at the tall boy from the mainland with increasingly adult eyes. Nor could she fail to be aware now of the man he had become. There was hardly a hint of the slender boy now in the broad shoulders and muscled arms. His skin was deeply tanned and his close cropped hair now curled crisply into his neck. Only his eyes, serious, slightly wary, were the same. She became aware that some sort of welcome back speech was called for, yet was unable immediately to re-establish that easy camaraderie they had shared all those years ago. He had been a boy then, around whom she had woven a romantic dream without so much as a touch of hands; a face in a crumpled snapshot propped up by her pillow whilst she waited for summer to return, not realising that it would not bring him this time. There had been letters; brief, stilted phrases in carefully formed handwriting which said nothing of her true feelings, and which, after the first few months, had petered out, forcing her to acknowledge that Matthew at his boarding school had other things with which to occupy his thoughts. And, since his father's death a short while ago, Matthew had been head of Corrigan Construction and further away from her world than ever.

"I was sorry to hear about your father's death," she murmured now.

Matthew's eyes flickered as he inclined his head in acknowledgment of her sentiments. Morwenna eyed him thoughtfully.

Had things improved between Matthew and his father over the years, she wondered? The glimpses she'd had of Ralph Corrigan on his infrequent visits to Inveree had filled her with awe, her childish mind comparing the impatient voice and forbidding features with the weather-beaten, keen gaze of her own fisherman father.

Matthew had made no secret of his animosity for his father, nor of his youthful contempt for the values of the world he moved in, apparently taking for granted the things it provided; public school education, the idyllic cottage retreat perched in the shelter of the cliffs a mile or so along the coast from the Beachcomber. Matthew glanced around the hallway now.

"So you came back," he commented drily at last. "And I thought you'd escaped."

His choice of words brought a swift response from Morwenna.

"Escaped?" Her tone was defensive. "That's a strange word to use. This is my home."

"Yet you left," he pointed out swiftly.

Morwenna looked at him almost

defiantly. "I went away to art school," she informed him. "Anyway, how do you know that?"

"Phil kept me informed of your achievements," he murmured.

"Really?" Unreasonable anger towards her absent brother rushed through her, yet when she spoke her tone was deceptively casual. "I didn't realise my progress was being monitored. Did he send you copies of my end of term reports, too?"

There was a flicker of amusement in Matthew's eyes which only served to increase Morwenna's annoyance.

"I was always an admirer of your artistic talents, Morwenna!" he responded gravely. "You were good. Even as a child of ten."

The unexpected praise should have pleased her yet the reference to the difference in their ages only goaded her further.

"But then a boy of—what—fifteen?—would hardly be a connoisseur of art," she couldn't resist saying.

A silence fell between them. This was ridiculous, Morwenna thought. She should have been delighted at his return, yet within minutes, they were in danger of quarrelling. And, she realised, it was his easy assumption of the right to question her about her life since he'd left which was irking her; or was it the fact that it had taken him so long to come back? If she were honest, wasn't that the main reason for the absurd annoyance which threatened to bubble over into downright anger?

She could see him in her mind's eye, standing in the bows of the boat on that last occasion, waiting to be taken back to the mainland, his eyes turned in their direction, his voice carrying clearly to Phil and herself, watching silently at the quayside.

"I'll be back next summer, you two. Don't forget me," he'd called. But he had not been back the following summer, though she acknowledged willingly that she had not been able to forget him.

"Why did you come back, Morwenna?" Matthew was eyeing her shrewdly now. "You had the talent, the best training. You could have gone on to great things. Yet here you are, minding the store again."

The unconscious irony in his tone evoked an instinctive flash of anger in her.

"I came back to nurse my father!" she

said icily. "He's very old and sick now. Nothing is as important as that, so far as I'm concerned. I'm afraid I must leave the adventuring to people like you and Phil."

Matthew eyed her contritely.

"I'm sorry. I didn't know your father was ill. How bad are things?" he asked.

Morwenna swallowed, her mind filling with images of the frail old man she had left upstairs only an hour ago.

"He probably won't live much longer," she murmured, her voice husky.

Matthew frowned.

"I'm sorry to hear that," he told her. He eyed her tentatively then. "I'd looked forward to having a chat with him," he ventured.

Morwenna gave him the ghost of a smile.

"He might not remember you," she said. "His memory comes and goes . . ." Her voice faltered.

"Nevertheless, I'd still like to visit him some time when he feels up to it," Matthew insisted. "I always got on well with him."

Smiling, Morwenna acknowledged the truth of his words. In many ways, the tall islander had been more of a father to Matthew than his own father had been. His fishing days behind him owing to ill-health, Tom Wainwright had been a familiar figure at the cottage Ralph Corrigan had bought for his family. And Morwenna could not deny that the burden of its maintenance throughout the winter had been a welcome source of income for a widower with two young children to support, and time on his hands.

An uneasy silence settled on them, which Morwenna made a conscious effort to dispel. Leaving the desk, she walked round towards Matthew.

"I'm forgetting my manners!" she said lightly. "And after not seeing you for so many years! Please come into the lounge, Matthew. Can I offer you anything—a drink, perhaps . . ."

"Thank you—no. Some other time, maybe," Matthew responded. "I ought to be getting back to Smugglers' Cottage—there's a lot to do to make it habitable again."

"You're opening it up again?" Morwenna asked.

"Why not?" He smiled briefly at her.

"It was my favourite place when I was younger. My father hasn't used it in recent years, but now it's mine, I'd like to spend more time here."

Morwenna eyed him hesitantly.

"Your company—"

"Has a competent board of directors to see to things when I'm not there," Matthew interrupted. His eyes held hers unwaveringly then. "Running Corrigan Construction isn't going to take over my whole life, Morwenna," he said after a moment. "There are other things. I had ambitions, too, if you recall. Not that I turned out to be very good as an artist; you were the talented one. But I have no intention of becoming the sort of person my father was, you can be sure of that."

Morwenna eyed him. So the old antagonism was still there—even though his father was dead. She looked away from his unflinching gaze.

"It will be like old times again," she said lightly. "If only Phil were here—"

Was it imagination—or had there been a slight stiffening of Matthew's figure at the mention of her brother?

"Does he come back often?" he asked.

She nodded. "At weekends. And I think he's due here for a spot of leave soon. It will be nice for you two to get together again, I imagine." She eyed him speculatively. "I was surprised when he left your firm, Matthew—" She broke off, becoming aware of Matthew's face. A shuttered look had come over it. He moved impatiently.

"Now that Phil's no longer with the firm, we don't really see anything of each other," he said stiffly.

He was obviously reluctant to be drawn on the subject. Morwenna stared at him, realising her earlier impressions had been correct. So their friendship had not stood the test of time! And yet they had been so close, here on the island. Was it true, as some people said, that once you left, becoming enmeshed with the harsh realities of the outside world, your personality changed? She herself, although content to be here, saw the island through more worldly-wise eyes since her time on the mainland. As for Phil, he was no longer the easygoing, unsophisticated boy he had once been. She'd noticed that, on his brief visits home. They had all been grateful to Ralph Corrigan for finding a place in his firm for Phil, once he'd left school. Unlike herself, Phil had been ambitious, hardly able to wait until he was old enough before leaving the island to make his way in the world. To all intents and purposes, he had been happy working at Corrigan Construction; then, inexplicably, he had left the firm shortly after Ralph Corrigan's death, finding a job with one of their competitors and offering no explanation for his sudden switch of allegiance. Indeed, he had evaded all her queries, making it obvious he did not wish to discuss the matter further. Now she could only surmise that there had been some kind of a quarrel between Matthew and Phil.

"Mm. St. Anselm's."

Brought back to the present by Matthew's voice, Morwenna followed his gaze to the wines and gifts placed for guests' convenience near to the reception desk.

"That's the local community of monks on the other side of the island," she explained. "You remember them, don't you?"

"Of course."

Picking up one of the bottles, he studied the label thoughtfully.

"And what else do the monks of St. Anselm's do, apart from making their own wine?"

"Oh, the usual things; souvenirs for tourists, that sort of thing. They like to keep the old crafts going. And they're self sufficient, too." Morwenna informed him. "They grow their own produce; in fact, we buy all our vegetables from them. There aren't many brothers left and they're finding it hard to manage. Like everyone else, they've had to adapt to the modern world and it isn't a calling which attracts many new recruits."

Replacing the bottle, Matthew stared through the window.

"Where did you say they live?"

"Over that way—" Morwenna pointed inland in a westerly direction towards a wooded valley, looking at Matthew in some bewilderment as she did so. Catching her eye, he shrugged.

"I'm just intrigued, that's all," he murmured. "People like that—they're almost part of a bygone age. I wouldn't mind visiting them some time. Is it a closed Order or would that be possible?"

"I don't know," Morwenna confessed. "Certainly they don't welcome women. They live in a large old house with extensive grounds which they use to full advantage; you couldn't exactly call it a monastery. Aunt Jessie is the only woman allowed into the place and that's only as far as the gatehouse to collect the vegetables. If you stop by the house, they'll let you have as much produce as you want, at a reasonable price."

"Thanks. I'll do that," Matthew responded. He continued to gaze out over the expanse of land for some moments.

"St. Anselm's," he murmured again, half under his breath.

He turned, becoming aware of Morwenna's puzzled gaze.

"So—Aunt Jessie's still here." He changed the subject quickly.

"Yes. Between us we manage to run the guest house and care for my father," Morwenna explained. "Though we don't have many guests, particularly at this late stage of the season."

Matthew's gaze was sympathetic.

"It can't be easy for the two of you," he murmured.

"We manage!" Morwenna said quickly.

If there was one thing she didn't want, she decided suddenly, it was pity from Matthew Corrigan. He sensed her change of attitude immediately.

"I'm sure you do!" His tone was conciliatory. "Does she still make those delicious cakes and scones I spent so much of my childhood scoffing?" he asked.

"She certainly does!" Morwenna's tone relaxed. "In fact, she's in complete charge of the kitchen. She's getting older now—can't move as quickly as she could."

"Is that why you came back?" Matthew asked shrewdly.

"Partly," Morwenna admitted. "Though to be honest, I was never all that happy on the mainland. I enjoyed my work but after a while, the island seemed to call me back. And once I knew father was so ill, I'd no regrets about leaving it all behind."

"A pity, though." Matthew's eyes rested on her face. "Hiding all that talent. Anyway—" he moved restlessly.

"Remember me to Aunt Jessie. I'll call in again to say hello to her."

"Yes, do!" Morwenna responded. "She'll be sorry to have missed you."

"And your father—don't forget I'd appreciate the chance of a chat with him when he's feeling up to it." Matthew turned towards the door, then hesitated, looking back at her. "It's good to see you again, Morwenna!" he said unexpectedly. "So many times I've wanted to return—they were good days . . ."

They stared at each other, and Morwenna was aware of a sudden warmth in her cheeks. Matthew's eyes had dropped to her ringless left hand resting on the top of the reception desk.

"There's no one . . . special in your life then?" The directness of his words took her by surprise. Her cheeks flaming, she shook her head, looking away in confusion.

The door opened suddenly, admitting a couple of the Beachcomber's guests, giving her time to regain her composure. When they had dispersed, she looked round to find that Matthew had slipped away unnoticed in the mêlée of exchanging greetings. Almost unconsciously, she moved to the half open front door, staring down the stony path to where Matthew's tall figure swung away towards the cliff road. It had been a short encounter, but one which left her in complete turmoil. She had not really expected to see Matthew Corrigan again, particularly after hearing of his father's death. So, after all, the idealistic boy had given in gracefully and followed in his father's footsteps, taking his place in that world he'd once so despised! Why had he returned after all this time? Did the island pull him back, as it did her? Art school had been more difficult than she'd expected, her enthusiasm seeming to diminish. Only when she was back on the island had it returned in full, making her realise that her instinct for capturing its wilderness in her painting was something which had slipped away once she left. Now, in her infrequent spare moments, she painted again, transferring the scenes before her to canvas. Had something like that happened to him, too? If so, why could he not have understood that by coming back here, she had gained, rather than lost something?

The boy Matthew would have understood, but the man obviously did not. It was peaceful here in a way the mainland would never be, but now that Matthew Corrigan was back, she had a feeling things were not going to remain so.

"Morwenna!" Hearing her name called, she turned to find her Aunt Jessie watching from the doorway. "Anything wrong?"

"No—" Closing the door, Morwenna retraced her steps. "Sorry, Aunt. Is there something you wanted? I was just about to start lunch preparations." Opening the kitchen door, Morwenna allowed her aunt to precede her.

"What do you think?" Her voice was light. "Matthew Corrigan's back on the island! He's just been in to say hello."

"Matthew Corrigan? After all this time?" The older woman looked at her in surprise. "I never thought we'd see the likes of him again. Didn't his father die recently?"

"That's right. Matthew intends to open up Smugglers' Cottage again, by the sound of things." Morwenna frowned. "Wasn't there a fire there or something? I can't recall much about it now."

"Yes. Some years ago. Someone—a tramp—was inside and died in the fire. They had the place patched up but never used it again, to my knowledge!" Aunt Jessie said thoughtfully. "Seems strange. You'd think Ralph Corrigan would have been glad to get the place off his hands, since his wife was too frail to use it much and the boy obviously outgrew it."

"Mm. Didn't sound like that to me. Matthew seemed keen to take up residence again," Morwenna ventured. Aunt Jessie eyed her sharply.

"Pity you didn't call me. I'd have enjoyed seeing him again," she said. "But then you were always the only one that boy had eyes for."

"That's nonsense!" Morwenna protested. "If the truth's known, he and Phil used to regard me as a bit of a nuisance, following them around the place. And he said he'd stop by later to say hello to you. He's keen to renew his friendship with Dad, too." Morwenna looked at the older woman in perplexity. "What do you think?"

"Mm. Might cheer him up," Aunt Jessie mused. "If he remembers him, that is, and provided he's having a good day."

Morwenna's face shadowed. Reaching for the basket of vegetables she began peeling them, and the two women worked in silence for a while, each busy with her own thoughts. Unsettled by Matthew Corrigan's unexpected appearance on the island, Morwenna found it difficult to concentrate on mundane tasks. Despite her firm contradiction of her aunt's earlier remarks, she couldn't resist a tingling of anticipation at the thought that he would be around for a while at least, and that he seemed keen to seek out old acquaintances. She looked up, studying her reflection in the mirror with critical eyes, smoothing her dark hair back from her forehead in an unconscious gesture. She was wearing hardly any make-up, preferring a more natural look, and her eyes, though fringed by dark lashes, were in her opinion a nondescript shade of grey. She thought for a moment of the women Matthew Corrigan must come into contact with in his life in the city; women who would be vying for his attention, even more so now that he was the owner of a sizeable construction company. It was hard to imagine there wouldn't be anyone special.

"There's nothing wrong with your looks, so stop fretting."

Despite the severity of her voice, Aunt Jessie's eyes were twinkling when Morwenna turned to look at her.

"Oh, I was just—"

"I know!" the older woman cut her embarrassed protests short, shooting her a shrewd glance. "Matthew Corrigan would be a fool if he didn't agree with me, too!" she added.

"Aunt Jessie—" Morwenna made no attempt to hide the rebuke in her voice this time. "Matthew and I haven't set eyes on each other for years—and there's a world of difference between us."

"There was when you were young but it didn't seem to matter then!" the older woman pointed out.

"We're not children any more." Morwenna's tone held a trace of asperity. "He just made a courtesy call for old times' sake, that's all. You're letting your imagination run away with you."

Placing the vegetables into pans, she left the kitchen and made her way into the dining room to set the tables, glad to escape the older woman's sharp eyes. The guest house was small, and apart from a village girl who came in twice a week to do the washing, they managed the work between them. It was a meagre existence but there was, for the moment, no other choice. Aunt Jessie would not have been able to care for her frail brother alone, even if they had given up the guest house.

After lunch, having a few moments to spare, Morwenna slipped upstairs to her father's bedroom. Opening the door, she peered inside. The old man was awake, his eyes flickering towards the door as he heard the sound of it opening. Tiptoeing to the bed, Morwenna squeezed his gnarled hand, resting on the counterpane. Her heart ached for the man who'd been mother and father to her for so many years. Blue eyes peered vacantly up at her, lips moved in a smile as he recognised her. Leaning over, Morwenna kissed the withered cheek, then smoothed the pillows behind his head.

"Thought you'd be asleep," she whispered in mock reproof.

"I'm not tired." Despite his assertion, the words obviously cost him an effort. Morwenna looked round the room. South facing, it allowed sunlight to stream in through the window, illuminating the old man's features and bringing a sudden lump to her throat. She hated to see him like this; the once tall, strong man who had been the centre of her life for so many years. With the onset of the crippling disease from which he suffered, he had quickly deteriorated into the shell she saw now. Some days, when the weather was good, he was able to sit in a chair in the garden or by the front door, watching the sea on which he had once earned his living, Other days, like today, he was content to remain in his bed.

"Matthew Corrigan's back on the island, Father." Leaning forward so that he could hear, Morwenna spoke more slowly than usual. "Do you remember him—the boy from Smugglers' Cottage up on the cliffs? You used to look after the cottage for his father—remember?"

Faded blue eyes focused on her face. He

frowned, struggling to take in her words. Watching him, Morwenna saw his eyes fill with inexplicable fear.

"Father?" She eyed him in sudden anxiety. "What is it?"

"No. They must not find out." His lips moved, forming the words. "The cottage —not find out—" He stopped, temporarily exhausted, his eyes closing. Morwenna watched him in foreboding.

"Are you feeling worse?" she asked gently.

"Not find out—" Each word was obviously an effort for him.

She eyed him watchfully, stroking his head in an attempt to soothe him.

"It's all right. There's nothing to worry about. You're safe, here with me and Aunt Jessie."

Settling his blankets around him, she waited until he dropped off into a light doze, then left the room, feeling vaguely disturbed as she hurried downstairs. He'd seemed so well yesterday. What had upset him so suddenly? Surely it couldn't have been her mention of Matthew Corrigan; she'd felt he only half understood what she was telling him, in any case. What shadows moved in his twilight world to cause him distress like that she had witnessed seconds ago? She sighed. If only there were more she could do for him, but the doctor had made it plain that all anyone could do now was make what remained of his life as comfortable as possible. A lump rose, unbidden, in her throat. Her youth was being wasted here on the island, despite what she had said to Matthew Corrigan about being happy to return. Her father was a beloved burden, and it was her privilege as well as her duty to care for him, but sometimes she wondered if her life would ever consist of anything else.

The rest of the day gave her no time to dwell on gloomy thoughts, as it was filled with activity. In no time it was drawing on towards evening and she was busy with meal preparations. The only guests at the moment were a few fishing enthusiasts and their wives. Several hotels had opened in recent years along the coast, and the Beachcomber tended to get only the odd straggle of guests at the lower end of the financial scale. Despite the scarcity of money Morwenna was thankful for the lack of guests, feeling they had more than enough to contend with at the moment.

The telephone shrilled and, aware that her aunt was busy elsewhere, Morwenna hurried across to it.

"Morwenna!"

Her heart raced as she recognised Matthew Corrigan's voice at the other end.

"Matthew! How are you?" She steadied her voice, anxious that he should not sense her involuntary pleasure at hearing him.

"I was wondering if you'd care to have a meal with me this evening—there must be a lot of news to catch up on," he was saying.

"Oh—I'm afraid I can't." There was genuine regret in her voice which she made no attempt to hide this time. "Aunt Jessie can't cope on her own."

"Oh." Matthew sounded disappointed, too.

There was a short, uncomfortable silence, then a solution presented itself.

"Why don't you come here for a meal?" Morwenna suggested. "It would give Aunt Jessie a chance to re-establish her culinary reputation with you."

"I'd like that." Matthew accepted

immediately making her wonder if this was what he'd been hoping she would say. She felt a tingle of pleasure surge through her.

"Good. We'll see you around eight o'clock then."

Replacing the telephone, she hurried to acquaint her aunt with the news that another place would need to be set. Busy with saucepans on the cooker, the older woman raised deceptively innocent eyes to her niece's face as she listened.

"My cakes and scones must have made a lasting impression on him for him to invite himself to dinner," she murmured.

"Oh, but he didn't . . ." Breaking off, Morwenna saw the twinkle in her aunt's eyes. "Really, Aunt Jessie," she remonstrated, shaking her head. "You're a rascal. I keep telling you he's just looking up old childhood friends."

Nevertheless, she dressed with care for dinner that evening, choosing a silky lemon dress she hadn't worn since her days on the mainland. Matthew arrived promptly at eight, a huge bunch of flowers in his hand for Aunt Jessie. After introductions had been made with the other guests, the meal was served. Aunt Jessie,

Morwenna noticed, had turned out one of her special recipes, though she vehemently denied it when Morwenna teased her about it. The meal was a friendly, informal one, Matthew chatting easily with the other guests. Morwenna found herself relaxing, aware too, that Matthew's eyes rested on her more frequently than was necessary. Aunt Jessie, she couldn't help noting with a smile, was completely won over by his charm.

"How much work have you managed on the cottage today?" Morwenna asked, as they lingered over coffee at the end of the meal.

"Not much," he confessed. "The electricity's restored and I've had a couple of men from the firm finishing off the plastering. The place is at least habitable now. And, as you'll have realised, I've had the telephone re-connected." He grinned mischievously. "I'm not as much of a recluse as all that. So I decided to go for a walk, having had enough of the cottage for one day. Matter of fact, I had a look at the monastic community down in the valley."

Out of the corner of her eye, Morwenna

studied him. He'd grown into a handsome man, she had to admit, with the easy self assurance of someone with his background and education. Catching sight of Aunt Jessie, his eyes followed her on her way upstairs with a laden tray for Tom Wainwright.

"How *is* your father, Morwenna?" he asked quietly, after a moment.

Her face shadowed. "Not too well today, I'm afraid." She forced cheerfulness into her voice. "Perhaps tomorrow he'll be brighter. I think he'll be pleased to see you when he's up to it."

"Good." Matthew's eyes narrowed. "And Phil—does he take his share of the responsibility when he comes over?"

"Yes, of course." Morwenna was instantly on the defensive. "Anyway—how did you enjoy your walk?" She changed the subject quickly. "Did you go inside the monks' residence?"

"No." The reply was rueful. "There was no one round the place, so I had a quick look from the garden." Aunt Jessie had returned and was now listening.

"They'd be at prayer, probably!" she

put in as she caught the gist of their conversation.

"Then I'm glad I didn't disturb them," Matthew said pleasantly. "I'll try again in a day or so."

Morwenna eyed him thoughtfully. The few elderly monks who comprised the St. Anselm's community seemed to have aroused an unwarranted amount of curiosity in Matthew.

"They don't welcome casual callers," Aunt Jessie informed him. "They live a very cloistered life. You could come with me if you like when I go to collect the vegetables," she offered, to Morwenna's surprise. "Do you have your car with you? It would make a welcome change from bringing the food home in a basket on my bicycle handlebars."

"I did bring the car over on the ferry." Matthew's eyes twinkled. "I'm at your service any time you need me, Ma'am."

Standing up, he looked at Morwenna, as the older woman moved away from them. "It's a beautiful evening. Walk me back down the lane?" he invited, smiling down at her.

"Leaving so soon?" Morwenna hid her

dismay behind a light tone. "Aunt Jessie will be disappointed."

"I'd hate to outstay my welcome," he countered lightly, extending a hand to her. "Coming?"

"I should help with the clearing up," she said uncertainly.

"Please." Matthew's voice was coaxing and she gave in gracefully. After making his farewells to Aunt Jessie Matthew stepped outside, Morwenna accompanying him. It was, as Matthew had said, a beautiful evening, after one of those fleeting last days which sometimes come in late summer. All too soon they had reached the point where the path divided, one side running up to the cliffs where Smugglers' Cottage perched, the other leading to the beach. Leaning against a huge boulder, Matthew looked upwards in the direction of the cottage.

"I can't tell you how glad I am to be using the cottage again," he said, smiling. "My father discouraged us from using it in the later years, despite the fact that it was completely restored after the fire." He eyed her questioningly. "Were you here then?"

"I don't recall much about it," Morwenna responded.

"It's such a good location," Matthew continued, turning to look at the cottage again, "particularly so with the hidden path which runs down to the beach. That came in handy when we were kids, didn't it?"

"It did," Morwenna agreed. Her eyes danced. "No doubt it came in handy for the smugglers of old, too. That's the reason it was named after them, wasn't it, the cottage? They brought their booty in quietly at night by sea, then transported it up to the cottage without anyone from the island seeing them."

"Neat!" Matthew observed drily. "I'll remember it, the next time I run out of baccy!"

They both laughed at that. Their eyes met and Morwenna looked away quickly, conscious of the colour which tinged her cheeks suddenly. They had, she realised, resumed their easy friendship of all those years ago without too much effort, and she had become aware, over the meal, of his growing attraction for her, the re-awakening of those half-formed feelings she'd had for him as a girl. For a moment she felt apprehension, aware that she was being drawn into something which she might not be ready for, yet would welcome, despite that. What kind of a man had Matthew Corrigan become? In many ways he was a stranger to her, yet at this moment it was as if they'd never been apart. He frowned suddenly.

"Morwenna . . ." The wary look she had noticed that morning was back in his eyes. "There's something—"

He broke off, interrupted by the noise of an approaching car engine. Both he and Morwenna turned instinctively, staring at the bright red, open topped car coming rapidly down the lane towards them. Morwenna heard Matthew's sharp intake of breath, yet paid no heed, her attention focused on the fair haired man sitting in the passenger seat beside the driver.

"Phil!" Delight broke over her features as the car stopped alongside them. "Why didn't you let me know you were coming?"

"Hello, Sis!"

Phil's lithe figure unwound itself from the front seat of the car. His smile faded as his eyes fell on Matthew and he acknowledged him curtly. Morwenna became aware then of the girl in the driving seat of the car. A stranger to her, she was breathtakingly beautiful, Morwenna saw that instantly. Her eyes took in the pale gold hair, the perfect, expertly made-up face. Elegant in well cut slacks and lemon sweater which accentuated the tones of her hair, the girl looked back at her calmly, aware of the effect she created. Matthew had stiffened at the newcomers' arrival, though he said nothing. The girl's eyes rested on him then in some amusement.

"Hello darling!" Her tone was light. "Phil didn't have his car, so I gave him a lift." Her eyes left Matthew's face to return to Morwenna's. "Aren't you going to introduce me?"

Realising then that the girl was not with Phil, Morwenna turned instinctively to look at Matthew. His expression was hard now, the easy intimacy of the last few minutes gone. He continued to stare silently at the girl, making no attempt to reply, and after a moment she shrugged and held out a languid hand towards Morwenna.

"Since Matthew has forgotten his manners, I'd better do it myself," she said. She was obviously enjoying the little scene, playing it out for full effect. "I'm April. Corrigan, that is. Mrs. Matthew Corrigan, to be exact."

2

MORWENNA was aware of an insistent voice within her, telling her she had no right to be angry —or even surprised. Matthew Corrigan had grown into an attractive man and it had been naïve of her to think he would still be free. Yet despite that, icy shock took hold of her, rapidly building itself into raging anger, though she was careful to give no outward sign of it. Her eyes remained fixed on the beautiful face of the woman in front of her, the mocking eyes waiting for her reaction. From somewhere within her, she drew reserves of dignity and self-control. Beside her, she saw Matthew's fists clench involuntarily; felt his anger, though he still hadn't spoken. Only Phil seemed unaware of the tension in the atmosphere. He would, Morwenna realised, have assumed that Matthew had told her about April. *Why hadn't he?* Why had he sought her out, re-awakening feelings in her she'd thought long dead, when he was not free to do so?

Anger was translating itself into pain now; sharp, undiluted pain which swamped her, threatening to reveal itself to the girl watching her.

"How do you do?" Forcing herself to speak naturally, Morwenna inclined her head, then without another glance at Matthew, linked her arm in her brother's. "To you goes the pleasure of escorting me back to the Beachcomber," she said lightly. "Aunt Jessie will be delighted to see you, Phil. 'Bye everyone!"

The last words were tossed carelessly over her shoulder as she drew Phil forward, towards the lane. She knew if she looked back, the naked pain in her eyes would be there for both Matthew and his wife to see. Deliberately concentrating her thoughts away from them, she walked determinedly away, hardly pausing for Phil to collect his luggage from the car and thank April for the lift before falling into step beside her. Aware now of her tension, he waited until they were out of earshot, before touching her arm briefly.

"Sorry, love. Did we arrive at a bad time?" he murmured.

Morwenna drew in her breath in an effort to steady her voice before she replied. "No Phil, it's not your fault. It's just that I hadn't realised—that is, Matthew hadn't said . . ." her voice wobbling, she broke off. Phil eyed her in concern.

"Our friend Matthew is no gentleman," he said wryly at last.

"There's no reason—I mean, why should he . . ." Stopping, Morwenna turned her head sharply away. Why indeed? And what right had she to feel so angry and hurt? He'd done nothing—said nothing—except renew an old acquaintanceship, as she herself had been at pains to stress to Aunt Jessie. If she had read more into his actions than that, it was hardly his fault. She was just someone to remember from long ago, whose company he'd sought out for old times' sake, feeling lonely in his cottage. She was a silly, sentimental fool to have thought otherwise. And yet there had been something in his eyes, lingering on her during their meal earlier, and, indeed, during that few moments on the cliff path before the others had arrived, which had stirred some response within her, evoking fleeting, adolescent memories and half formed feelings—feelings a man with a wife had no right whatsoever to pry into. And April looked every inch his wife, Morwenna had to admit. Elegant, graceful, with an air of sophistication no island girl could have, April would be as out of place on Inveree as Morwenna herself had felt in the city. The sort of girl who would look right beside a man in Matthew Corrigan's position. Anger burned through Morwenna. Were they exchanging confidences, laughing at her behind her back now, those two?

Aware that she was walking so quickly even Phil's long legs had difficulty keeping up, she slowed down.

"Feeling better?" Her brother eyed her shrewdly as he reached her side.

"He ought to have told me." Morwenna breathed hard, her eyes glinting. Anger was taking over again, dulling the pain.

"Those kind of people don't do the things they ought," Phil observed. Turning, he stared behind him into the distance. "And why April's come here to the island, I don't know. He's made it obvious he doesn't want her company. Nor does he deserve it."

Stopping, Morwenna looked at him. "You didn't meet her on the ferry, did you?" she asked. "You already knew her."

"Oh, April and I go back a long way!" Phil responded easily. "Long before she married Matthew, of course!" he was quick to add. He eyed his sister thoughtfully. "You don't know the story, of course. April came to live at the Corrigans' home some years ago; she and Matthew practically grew up together, in fact. She was the daughter of one of Ralph Corrigan's employees. When she was left an orphan, Ralph Corrigan, like the philanthropist he was, took her into his family, paid for her education, the lot!" His tone was dry. "I hadn't realised they'd decided to make the arrangement a permanent one, though why she chose him out of all the men she could have had, I'll never know."

Conscious of the underlying bitterness in his tone, Morwenna eyed him. Was he one of those men, she wondered shrewdly?

"Why did you say that about Matthew

not wanting her to come here?" she enquired.

"Oh—" Phil shrugged. "He seems to have more time for his business than he has for her." He gave Morwenna a sombre look. "Our little island boy has, I'm afraid, become just like his father. Using people, manipulating them to suit his own ends."

Morwenna frowned. Phil's words seemed oddly at variance with the impression she had formed on meeting Matthew Corrigan again. Noting her expression, Phil tucked his arm inside hers as they neared the door of the Beachcomber.

"Cheer up, love!" he said gently. "You're well out of it. He's not your kind."

Angrily Morwenna pulled away from him.

"There's nothing between me and Matthew; why does everyone keep assuming there is?" she demanded. "Good heavens, we only met again today for the first time in years! But I can't help feeling angry that he didn't tell me he was married. He's been to the guest house twice today, after all." Making a visible effort to calm herself, she walked in front of Phil, pushing open the front door.

"How's Dad, by the way?" Following her into the house, Phil looked at her enquiringly.

Morwenna's face took on a troubled expression.

"He didn't seem too well earlier," she admitted.

"I'll go up right away."

Putting his suitcase down in the hallway, Phil turned towards the stairs. Eyeing his luggage, Morwenna called out after him.

"How long are you here for?" she asked.

Turning, he flashed her a smile. "I may stay a week or two. What better place is there to spend a summer holiday than at home?"

Morwenna's heart lifted slightly. "It will be nice to have you here for a while," she told him.

"It will be nice to be here for a while," he responded, on his way upstairs.

Smiling absently, Morwenna went in search of Aunt Jessie. The lounge was empty, but the fire which had been lit in the hearth cast a welcoming glow as she entered. The last few minutes had unnerved her and she was glad to slip unobserved into an armchair, grateful for the chance to be alone. Despite her brave words to Phil, she acknowledged to herself now that the unexpected arrival of Matthew Corrigan's wife had upset her unduly. She had allowed herself to become lulled into a romantic dream over the last few hours and April Corrigan's arrival had been the jolt she needed to back away before any great harm was done. But still the question gnawed at her. Why *hadn't* Matthew told her he was married? She recalled his sharp intake of breath when he saw the car approaching them. He had obviously not expected his wife to come to Inveree. Had he been hoping to indulge in a summer dalliance with Morwenna to liven up the tedium of life at Smugglers' Cottage, in the absence of his wife? Morwenna's face flamed. Is that how he had seen her, a momentary diversion? He was, after all, a stranger to her now. How did she know what kind of man he was?

The friend and confidant of those childhood days had gone for ever.

She moved restlessly in her chair. When would she learn not to be so trusting? Why hadn't she understood that a man like Matthew Corrigan moved in different circles—and always had done? It had not been apparent to her as a child, but now she was an adult and the child's naïvety ought to have been swept away long ago. People like she and her family were there just to serve people like Matthew Corrigan! Morwenna's eyes flashed. Matthew did not have to explain himself to her if he chose not to—but neither, she vowed firmly, did she have to be made a fool of twice by him. For he *had* made a fool of her, using her aunt's hospitality to further his own ends. It would not happen again.

The door opened and she heard Phil's voice calling her.

"Here, Phil!"

Raising herself up in the chair, she peered round at him, determinedly banishing her dark mood. Phil's eyes were narrowed as he moved further into the room and dropped into the chair opposite her.

"How was Dad?" she asked.

"He seemed a bit confused," Phil responded. "I'd go so far as to say afraid, until he realised who I was. Strange." He shook his head thoughtfully. Watching him, Morwenna felt a sense of disquiet enveloping her. She had convinced herself, over the last few weeks, that her father was a little better, but now . . . Her face shadowed. Was the end nearer than she had thought?

"Aunt Jessie—hello!"

At Phil's pleased exclamation, Morwenna turned to see her aunt entering the room, her face creased in a welcoming smile for her nephew.

"So the prodigal returns!" The affectionate way in which she said it belied the severity of her words.

Phil's face assumed an exaggerated grimace. "Don't rush out to kill the fatted calf just yet, darling aunt," he told her. "There's plenty of time. I had a few days' leave coming and decided to spend it here. So line up any wood cutting, coal carrying or general donkey work you've been saving for me."

Morwenna gave him an amused glance.

"We do manage to stagger along when you're not here," she said, "But it is nice to have you home, if only for a short time. Why didn't you let us know you were coming?"

"Oh, it was one of those spur of the moment decisions, Wenny!" he replied, using his childhood nickname for her. "I heard a whisper that our overlord was heading this way, so thought it wouldn't do any harm to keep an eye on him; see what he's up to."

"Overlord?" Aunt Jessie eyed him blankly. "Whatever are you talking about, Phil?"

Phil's eyes lingered on his sister's face.

"Ask Morwenna," he murmured. "She knows who I mean."

Morwenna had turned away at his words. "I think Phil is referring to Matthew Corrigan, Aunt," she said at last. "Though why he should say that, I don't know."

"No?" Phil's eyebrows lifted expressively. "You haven't heard what the locals

—and others—call this place?" His voice hardened. "Did I ever tell you what the guy I had to report to said to me, the first morning I went to work for Corrigan Construction? 'Oh yes—you're the kid from Corrigan's Island, aren't you?'" His eyes smouldered. "That was the first time I heard it but I soon came to realise how appropriate it was."

Morwenna looked at him in irritation. "That's nonsense," she protested. "None of the Corrigans have been here for years and they didn't intrude when they were here. In fact, quite a few people in this place have reason to be grateful to Matthew's father—you included."

"Oh yes—we're all bought and paid for!"

Phil's tone was flippant but there was an unaccustomed bitterness in it which made Morwenna eye him sharply.

"What happened between you and Matthew Corrigan?" Her voice held a challenging note. "Why did you leave the firm as soon as he took over?"

Phil moved restlessly. "That's not up for discussion," he said briefly. "Suffice it to say I'm happier under a new master. And I owe Matthew Corrigan nothing."

There was vehemence in his voice. Morwenna's gaze was troubled as she looked at him. Whatever had caused the rift, it would not easily be healed. For a moment she wished heartily that Matthew Corrigan had not come back to Inveree. His return seemed to have stirred up a welter of hidden feelings which would have been better left submerged.

She spent a restless night despite her natural fatigue, her mind running over the events of the day. Her father had seemed in a calmer state of mind when she had helped him to bed, yet she herself slept fitfully. Leaving her bed, she padded across to the open window and breathed in the fresh air. The moon was bright, illuminating the scene before her, and her eyes strayed against her will to the spot on the cliffs where Smugglers' Cottage perched. A light burned in a downstairs window, as she watched. Which of them was awake, besides herself, at this time of night? Sighing, she returned to her bed. Whoever it was, it was no business of hers.

Thoughts of Matthew Corrigan seemed

to dominate Morwenna's mind the following morning, despite her efforts to shrug them away. It seemed the feelings she'd begun to form for him as a child, though lying dormant all these years, were stronger than she had realised.

"Hello there."

In the act of polishing the Beachcomber's brass door knocker, Morwenna turned at the sound of a voice, to find herself staring at April Corrigan. Dressed in well fitting jeans and brightly coloured top, her hair swept up in an elegant pony tail, she looked exquisite. She eyed Morwenna, a slight smile on her lips. Angry at allowing herself to be caught at a disadvantage, Morwenna's hands tightened over the duster she was holding.

"Good morning." She tried unsuccessfully to inject some warmth into her voice.

Aware of it, April seemed amused.

"Morwenna, isn't it?" Her voice was cool. "I was in the village shopping and thought I'd pay a call on Phil," she went on pleasantly. "Is he around, by any chance?"

"April!" Phil's voice sounded behind them before Morwenna could reply.

Turning, she saw him standing by the front door, smiling in April's direction.

"Oh, there you are!" She eyed him provocatively. "When can I look forward to the sailing trip you promised me?"

"Why not now?" he returned promptly. "That's if there's nothing more I can help with?" He looked enquiringly at Morwenna. "I've done all the jobs which needed doing."

Morwenna shook her head, then aware that April was eyeing her speculatively, made an effort at cordiality.

"Off you go and enjoy yourself," she told Phil. "It's your holiday, after all." She smiled in April's direction. "What do you think of our island, now you've seen a little more of it?" she enquired politely.

April shrugged. "It's quite pretty," she conceded. "And that cottage—it's so quaint!" She gave a low, amused laugh. "Thank heavens Matthew's civilising it." She ended with an exaggerated shudder.

At the mention of Matthew Corrigan, the atmosphere seemed to recharge.

"How *is* our lord and master this morning?" Phil asked.

"Oh, Phil—you are naughty!" Despite

her reproving words, April was obviously amused by his sarcasm. "He's been out for hours, actually," she continued. "I don't know what he's looking for—but it kept him from coming to bed for ages."

Morwenna averted her head from the other woman's gaze, sensing that the remark had been made for her benefit.

"You didn't walk here from the cottage?" Phil was regarding April in mock horror.

"Oh no—I left the car in the main street," April answered. "It will be all right until I return, won't it?"

"No one will touch it!" Unaccountably irritated by the remark, Morwenna sprang to the defence of the island people before Phil had a chance to reply.

"Good!" April's eyes danced as she turned to Phil. "Then what are we waiting for, Phil?" Taking his arm, she smiled up into his face. "Oh, by the way—" Turning she pointed in the direction of the small cove below Smugglers' Cottage. "There's a beautiful waterfall there; I can hear it gushing, from my window. Is it part of Corrigan property?"

"Oh, you mean Lovers' Point." Phil's

eyes had followed her pointing finger. "As for being part of Corrigan property, I thought the whole island came under that definition!"

"Phil!" Unable to stop herself, Morwenna spoke sharply. "What a ridiculous thing to say!" Aware of April's interested glance, she turned back to her work, wishing she had restrained herself from speaking.

Phil ignored his sister's rebuke. "It's a local beauty spot, actually," he mused, still staring in the direction of the cove. "Isn't there a legend it takes its name from, Wenny?" Turning, he eyed his sister and reluctantly she allowed herself to be drawn back into the conversation.

"Yes. It happened a long time ago," she informed them. "I can't recall too much of it, though it concerned two members of the smugglers' ring, I think. One man was in love with another man's wife. There was a fight, up there near the waterfall. One of them—the lover—fell to his death and the other one, grief-stricken at what he'd done to his friend, turned on the woman who'd been the cause of it all, hurling her over the edge from that point. He himself was hanged for the murder."

"What a tragic tale!" April repressed a shiver, "and I suppose the spot is haunted now?"

Aware of the other woman's amused scepticism, Morwenna didn't reply for a moment.

"When the wind is high," she murmured at last, "some people say they can hear the woman moaning for her lost love."

"Oh dear." April pulled a face and looked at Phil. "I think we'd better go before this gets any sadder. Where's the boat, Phil?"

"It's kept moored down by the jetty," Phil informed her. He eyed her clothes dubiously. "You'll need some warmer clothes, I think. Perhaps you've an anorak that would fit, Morwenna?" He eyed her questioningly.

Going into the house, Morwenna took a jacket from the hallway cloakstand and handed it to Phil, who wrapped it round April's shoulders. Then, amid much laughter and chatter, they moved off in the direction of the harbour. Morwenna watched them silently. Even in the shapeless jacket, April cut an elegant figure, making Morwenna more aware than ever of her carelessly donned sweater and jeans. She gave the door knocker an unusually vigorous rub, then went inside the house, feeling vaguely disquieted. Why wasn't Matthew Corrigan taking his wife sailing, she thought with sudden asperity? Drawing a comb through her hair, she surveyed her reflection in the mirror, mentally comparing her thick, chestnut locks with the silvery ones of April Corrigan.

"Morwenna!"

Turning at the sound of the voice, she saw Matthew Corrigan watching her from the open doorway. He made an apologetic gesture.

"I rang the bell, but no one answered."

"I'm sorry—I turned it off whilst I polished the door knocker. I must have forgotten to turn it back on . . ." Morwenna's voice trailed away. Angry at herself for being caught again at a disadvantage, she made an effort to compose herself.

"You just missed your wife—she's gone

sailing with Phil," she said, a distant note creeping into her voice.

Matthew made an impatient movement. "I wasn't looking for April—I came to see you," he said.

"Oh." Morwenna eyed him steadily. "Can I do something for you?" There was a formal note in her voice which was not lost on him. He stared at her frowningly.

"Can I sit down for a moment?" He nodded in the direction of a chair.

"Yes, of course. Would you like some coffee?" Morwenna stepped back as he advanced into the room.

"Thank you—no. I just thought, well—that some sort of an explanation was called for."

"Oh?" Morwenna was rapidly gaining control of herself, the icy anger of yesterday coming to the front of her mind. Unconsciously she clenched her hands by her side, keeping her voice steady when she spoke. "Explanation of what?"

Matthew eyed her soberly. "I don't blame you for being angry," he said at last.

"I'm not angry, Matthew—why should I be?" In spite of her words, there was an edge to Morwenna's voice which she couldn't hide.

Matthew shrugged. "I should have told you right at the start," he said at last.

Turning, Morwenna picked up some magazines and stuffed them into the rack. Keeping her hands busy helped control her rising emotions and gave her an excuse to keep her face averted from Matthew Corrigan's gaze.

"No explanations are necessary, Matthew!" she said at last.

"I think there are," he said quietly. He watched her efforts at tidying for a few seconds. "Morwenna, would you stop that and listen to me for a moment?" he asked abruptly.

Anger flamed into Morwenna's cheeks. She recalled her brother's taunting comments about Matthew Corrigan, the way he'd referred to him as their "lord and master". The memory, together with the sharpness of Matthew's tone, had an immediate and inevitable effect.

"Please don't give me orders in my own house," she said, facing him. Twin spots of colour tinged Matthew's cheeks.

"It wasn't an order, Morwenna!" he

said evenly, "I asked for time to make an explanation—"

"And I told you—no explanation is necessary!" Morwenna's swiftly mounting anger belied her words, yet now she made no attempt to stem it. "Your personal life has nothing to do with me—"

"Morwenna—" His voice grim, Matthew caught at her arm. "Please listen to me! I was going to tell you last night, just before they arrived. It had been such a lovely evening—I hated to spoil it . . ."

"By remembering you had a wife?" Morwenna was unable to resist the jibe, despite her previous efforts to keep the conversation on an impersonal level.

Matthew flinched at the harshness of the words. "I never for one moment forgot I had a wife!" he said stiffly.

Letting go of her arm, he stepped back. "Since you're not prepared to allow me to explain," he continued in a tight voice, "there's no point in continuing this conversation."

Turning, he walked out of the room, leaving Morwenna staring after him. Shaking with anger, she made a visible effort to control herself. Shutting the door, she buried her face in her hands, feeling their coolness against her hot cheeks. The encounter had shaken her to the depths, yet hadn't she been unconsciously awaiting it, knowing it would come? Things could not have been left the way they were between Matthew and herself. He was right, some sort of explanation was called for. Yet what explanation could there be, other than that he had not expected April to turn up on the island, and therefore Morwenna would not have known of her existence until and unless he chose to tell her?

Hearing the clinking of cups from the kitchen, Morwenna hurried through to help. The few guests staying at the Beach-comber tended to leave early in the morning for a day's fishing or walking, so that she and Aunt Jessie were free until it was time to prepare the evening meal.

"Coffee?" Aunt Jessie's eyes glinted at Morwenna from behind her spectacles, taking in the flushed cheeks. "I thought I heard voices." She eyed her niece questioningly.

"Yes." Morwenna's voice trembled. "Matthew Corrigan called in for a moment. He was looking for his—for his wife. She arrived last night."

"So he's married." Aunt Jessie's voice was casually noncommittal.

"Yes." Morwenna forced a lighter tone into her voice. "So your matchmaking plans came to nothing, after all."

"I knew there was something troubling him." The older woman's voice was reflective.

Making no reply, Morwenna helped herself to a cup of coffee, then headed for the door as quickly as she could. She was in no mood, after her recent encounters with Matthew and April, for Aunt Jessie's gentle probing.

"Did he say any more about visiting your father?" Aunt Jessie's voice halted her on her way out. "Your father was talking about him this morning, that's why I ask."

Morwenna turned, looking at her in surprise. "Dad, talking about Matthew? So he did understand me yesterday!"

"He understood all right!" Aunt Jessie responded.

"What did he say?" Morwenna asked.

Pulling the plug from the sink, the older

woman dried her hands on the towel, before replying. "He said—'Has the Corrigan boy left the island yet? You must make him leave.' Now why do you suppose he said that?" She eyed Morwenna speculatively.

Morwenna shook her head in bewilderment. "Matthew always got on well with Dad. I'd have thought he would have been pleased to see him again. I'll go up to him—"

"He's asleep now." Aunt Jessie said quickly. "Don't disturb him. Why *has* Matthew Corrigan come back, after all this time?" She darted a shrewd glance at her niece.

"So far as I know, he's renovating the cottage in order to spend more time here," Morwenna informed her. "If there is any other reason, I don't know what it is. Maybe, now he's head of Corrigan Construction, he has an even greater need for a place where he can escape the pressures of the job," she continued thoughtfully. "He always loved Inveree's peace."

"Well, his coming back doesn't seem to have done much for anybody's peace here at the Beachcomber," Aunt Jessie observed. "He seems to have had an effect on all three of you, in the short time he's been here."

Morwenna felt the colour returning to her cheeks. "Nonsense!" she said lightly. "We just lead such a quiet existence here that any newcomer makes an impression."

"Mm." The other woman touched her arm sympathetically. "I know it's not much of a life here for you," she murmured. "If you wanted to go back—"

"I don't!" Morwenna answered her quickly. "This is where I belong—I'm happy here." Yet, despite her words, she realised with a sinking heart that there was no denying the serenity of her life on Inveree had been irrevocably disturbed by Matthew Corrigan's return . . .

Later, feeling restless, Morwenna decided to go for a walk. There were times when the atmosphere in the house depressed her and at such times she was apt to take her sketch book and head for the cliffs, to spend a quiet hour sketching some aspect of her island home. From the cliffs she had a vantage point over the whole of this side of the island. Finding a comfortable spot she curled up in the shelter of an overhanging rock and proceeded to draw the scene before her, her good humour gradually returning as she did so. At times like this, she wondered why she had ever left to go to the mainland. An object, moving quickly, caught her eye and she realised it was a car, moving down the cliff path below her, heading inland towards the wooded valley some miles away. Her pen poised above her sketch book, she watched the car's progress, realising it belonged to Matthew Corrigan. She recalled his intention of visiting the monks of St. Anselm's. What was there in the monastic community which held such fascination for him, she wondered again? Picking up her belongings, she left to return to the Beachcomber, her concentration lost.

He made no attempt to contact her again over the following days and she was thankful for the respite. She'd always endeavoured to be honest with herself, and tried now to analyse the impact Matthew Corrigan and his wife had made on her emotions. She had, she admitted to herself, felt a resurgence of the old attraction, but it was a situation, once acknowledged, she felt she could face and deal with. Any attraction she had felt for him, she told herself firmly, had been swallowed up in the aftermath of her anger at his deception. And there were other things to occupy her. Her father had seemed to settle down in the days which followed Matthew Corrigan's return, but the piquancy of the situation engendered by the arrival of Matthew's wife at the same time as Phil—and the fact that they seemed to have known each other in earlier days—had a disquieting effect on Morwenna. They seemed to spend more time than was appropriate in each other's company, yet she could only watch in growing anxiety. Though her frequent glimpses of April Corrigan had hardly been sufficient for her to form a judgment of the woman's character, Morwenna's own intuition told her that she was a potential source of trouble. Seeking Phil out deliberately, she couldn't fail to be aware of Morwenna's disapproval, yet chose to ignore it. It was a situation charged with danger, Morwenna felt; a classic example of the other man, flattered by the attentions of a bored wife, neglected by a husband seemingly immersed in his own affairs. It boded no good for any of them. Several times Morwenna attempted to draw Phil on the subject, only to retreat at the last moment. Was she reading more into the situation than she should, she asked herself, as Phil and April set off on another of their jaunts? They were old friends, and if Matthew didn't mind, why should she take it upon herself to pass moral judgment? Yet the danger of the situation tormented her until she had to speak. She chose a time when Phil had just returned from one of the sailing trips which seemed to have found such favour with April. Choosing her words carefully, Morwenna tackled him.

"You seem to be spending a fair amount of time with Mrs. Corrigan," she began tentatively.

"What does that mean?" Phil raised questioning eyes from the magazine he had picked up, after flopping down into the chair.

Morwenna frowned and looked away from him. "It's just that I'd hate you to become involved in something which may become unpleasant," she said at last.

"Oh? You think April and I are having an affair?" Phil asked.

Despite the lightness of his tone, Morwenna sensed the anger behind it.

"She *is* married to Matthew," she pointed out.

"So she is. Not that he seems to be aware of it," Phil responded.

"That's hardly your business," Morwenna insisted.

Phil sighed, and put down the magazine he'd been reading. "April and I are not having an affair, darling sister," he said patiently. "Though one could hardly blame her if we were, the way that oaf neglects her."

"How do you know that? He's probably very busy!" Morwenna protested. "I'm not trying to lecture you, Phil—but I think you should consider very carefully whether you're being used."

"Oh come on, Wenny!" Phil looked at her in exasperation. "You've disliked April from the moment you set eyes on her—and we don't have to look far to find the reason for that!"

Morwenna felt her temper rising. "We

were discussing you and April," she said quietly.

"Wrong. *You* were discussing me and April!" Phil snapped. "You don't understand, Morwenna. You've spent too much time on this island. But even you should have realised that Matthew and April lead separate lives."

"Oh? They have a modern marriage, according to your definition?" Morwenna countered.

Phil shrugged. "Call it what you like. Matthew Corrigan doesn't care what his wife gets up to," he stated. "He deserves to lose her, the way he treats her. And I'll tell you something else. Whatever reason he may have given you for coming back here, he's lying. Matthew Corrigan is here for a definite purpose."

"What purpose could he have?" Morwenna looked at him uncertainly.

"I don't know." Phil eyed her grimly. "But he does own a construction company—and this is the sort of place people like him exploit, unless they're stopped."

Morwenna stared at him in growing dismay. "You mean—he plans to build here? But what?"

"I've just said—I don't know," Phil said. "A holiday camp, perhaps? There's plenty of scope here, if that's the sort of thing you want."

"Holiday camp?" Morwenna's eyes opened in horror. "Here—on Inveree? But that would ruin it! And Matthew always said the thing he liked most about Inveree was its unspoilt peace . . ."

Even as she spoke, she was recalling the day she had seen Matthew Corrigan driving out towards the monastic community of St. Anselm's. A picturesque, wooded valley like the one they lived in would be a prime target for unscrupulous profiteers—and the uprooting of a few elderly monks would mean nothing to such people.

"That was a long time ago," Phil was saying. "You're not dealing with an idealistic boy now, Morwenna. Matthew Corrigan is a man—a ruthless man. He got rid of me quickly enough—more or less told me to find another job the day his father died."

"Got rid of you?" Morwenna's voice was almost a whisper.

"Yes. So if you have any idea that a man

like Matthew Corrigan would hesitate to move in on this island, forget it!" Phil's voice was bitter. "It's not known as Corrigan's Island for nothing! Before long, Wenny, this place will be awash with day trippers, fun fairs, and holiday complexes. Our beautiful island will be ruined—and when that day comes, you'll have Matthew Corrigan to thank for it!" With a savage movement, he rose from his chair and swung out of the room, leaving Morwenna to stare after him in horror.

3

"IS it true what Phil says? Is that the reason you're here—to build some—" Morwenna's hand swept upwards in a contemptuous movement—"some *holiday complex* on our island?"

Face flushed with anger, she confronted Matthew by the side of his car. He had been about to climb in and drive away, but, noting her approach, had waited.

It was barely an hour since Phil had made his prediction about the reason for Matthew Corrigan's return to Inveree. Even now, Morwenna could hardly believe that was what Matthew intended to do. Yet it all fitted together; his unexpected return after recently taking over Corrigan Construction, the modernising of the old family cottage, and—most important of all—the interest that he had shown in the monastic community in the valley. By far the most scenic part of the island, it would be the ideal spot for such an enterprise—if that's what it could be called, Morwenna thought bitterly. To her, the idea of establishing a holiday complex on Inveree represented the biggest blow against conservation in the area, the most mindless act of commercial vandalism she had heard of—and not the kind of thing she would ever have connected with Matthew Corrigan. Yet, according to Phil, that was exactly what Matthew intended to do—and he had not even had the honesty to announce his intentions openly. But then, honesty had not been one of his strong points since his arrival, Morwenna recalled angrily. The realisation that this was the second unpleasant shock connected with Matthew Corrigan in a few days had been one of the factors which had goaded her into this impulsive action. Hardly stopping to think after her conversation with Phil, she had grabbed her coat and left the Beachcomber, heading in the direction of Smugglers' Cottage, her fury mounting with each step she took. Seething with anger, she had made her way up to the cliff path, her feet flying along the ground seemingly of their own accord, her fists clenched inside the pockets of her coat.

Catching sight of Matthew outside the

cottage door, she had increased her pace, determined on a show down. A head on clash between them, she realised now, had been inevitable. She could not remember when she had last felt so angry. It was as if Matthew had betrayed not only her family but also the memory of the boy she had known many years ago. A boy, she thought bitterly now, who would have viewed the prospect of a holiday complex on the island with as much horror as she did.

Matthew was staring at her now, obviously surprised by her sudden appearance at the cottage, full of outraged indignation. The merest flicker of amusement showed in his eyes.

"Do you always believe what Phil tells you, Morwenna?" he asked now, a trace of mockery in his voice.

Colour flooded into Morwenna's cheeks as she faced him. "Shouldn't I?" she challenged. "I asked you a question, Matthew. You haven't answered it yet."

A flicker of annoyance crossed his features and he moved restlessly. "I wasn't aware I had to account for my movements to you," he said at last.

His remark only infuriated Morwenna further. Her eyes glinted. "If what Phil says is true, you'll be accountable to everyone living on this island before long!" she flung at him. "Do you think we'll just stand by and let you spoil it?"

"Would it be spoiling it?" Matthew quirked an eyebrow at her. "Done with taste, it might actually be an asset to the island, not to mention the extra employment and prosperity."

Morwenna's face whitened at this apparent confirmation of what Phil had forecast. "So it *is* true!" she whispered, staring at him in unbridled horror. "I can hardly believe that you—*you*—would do such a thing—"

Matthew glanced at her keenly, noting her nearness to tears. "I didn't say that," he defended himself quickly.

"Well, what *are* you saying?" Hope flooded back into Morwenna's eyes. Perhaps things were only at a tentative stage after all and Matthew could be influenced to change his mind.

His face wore an exasperated expression now. "I've already said—I don't have to tell you my reasons for coming back to Inveree!" he said crisply.

Morwenna stared at him. "You can't just leave me hanging around!" she exclaimed. "Either tell me you *are* planning some kind of complex here—or deny it, for heaven's sake!"

Matthew opened the door of the car. "As I've said—I don't have to answer to you or your brother." His voice was hard. "Now, if you don't mind, Morwenna, since this is obviously not a social call and it would therefore be a waste of time asking you inside for coffee, I'd like to leave to keep an appointment. Can I give you a lift as far as the Beachcomber?"

Morwenna stared at him in amazement. "You have grown up into the most high-handed, arrogant man I've ever met!" she said unsteadily at last.

A slow flush spread over Matthew's face and his mouth set grimly. "You're entitled to your opinions," he said icily. "But what you are not entitled to do, Morwenna, is question me about my personal affairs."

"It's our affair, too!" Morwenna protested. "You're going to spoil our island—the island which you loved so much once . . ." her voice wobbled dangerously, before trailing off. To her horror, she realised how near she was to tears. It came to her then that finding out about Matthew's marriage had upset her far more than she had allowed herself to believe. On top of that came the revelations of what he might be planning for Inveree. To think she had cherished sentimental memories of this man! There was nothing of the idealistic boy left in him; in his place was, by all accounts, a ruthless business man who thought nothing of trampling over the feelings of anyone who opposed his wishes.

He was watching her warily now, aware of her threatening tears. "You really have no right to interrogate me like this, Morwenna," he said in a gentler voice, "particularly on the basis of an unfounded accusation of Phil's."

Making a superhuman effort to control her emotions, Morwenna eyed him.

"Can you give me your word you aren't planning to build some kind of complex here?" she challenged.

Matthew looked away from her. "I've

told you. I'm not prepared to answer that," he said firmly.

Morwenna's fists clenched by her sides. "If you won't deny it, I will have to assume that what Phil says is correct," she retorted.

His eyes flickered momentarily. "Believe what you like," he said tersely. "Now—how about that lift?"

"I think you should know—" Morwenna walked round the car to face him. "That our family will do all we can to oppose you."

"As you like!" His tone was sardonic. "At least it will give your brother something to do instead of chasing other men's wives around."

"I think you've got that the wrong way round, haven't you?" Morwenna responded furiously. "Ever since she arrived, your wife has been playing up to Phil—"

"Yes, she's rather good at that, isn't she?" Matthew countered drily. "Though Phil isn't exactly putting up much resistance, is he?"

"Doesn't it bother you?" Morwenna regarded him helplessly. "April's making you look ridiculous! Why don't you do something about it?"

She was aware that the conversation had taken too personal a turn, yet she was too angry to care. All she wanted to do at that moment was needle him, knock that infuriating gleam of amusement from his eye. The jibe went home. Matthew's mouth tightened.

"The state of my marriage is my affair, Morwenna!" he snapped. "But if you must know, I don't really give a damn what my wife does—or who she does it with!"

The words hung on the air. Morwenna regarded him in frowning bewilderment. What kind of a man had Matthew Corrigan become in the intervening years since she had seen him last? A man who allowed his wife to humiliate him, yet who apparently was not prepared or interested enough to take any action. Matthew was speaking again, some of the anger gone from his voice.

"April and I lead separate lives, Morwenna!" he said quietly. "That's all I'm prepared to say. Now, for the last time, do you want that lift or not?"

He held the car door open but Morwenna shook her head, stepping back.

"I don't think I want to be seen with you!" she said abruptly.

Turning away, she walked down the path. She heard Matthew's exasperated sigh, the slam of the car door, then seconds later, the car roared past her down the slope. Hunching herself into her jacket, Morwenna turned miserably towards home, dejection apparent in every part of her. What had this impulsive visit achieved? Nothing—except to leave her even more mystified and angry than before. Matthew's refusal to deny or confirm Phil's accusation could only be interpreted one way. He *was* planning something for the island—and his reluctance to talk about it meant he knew only too well how the locals would view such an enterprise.

Morwenna glanced instinctively to her left down to the wooded valley, picturing it filled with uniform chalets and—she shuddered—a fairground, even? How could he even consider it; he, who'd loved the island for its unspoilt beauty? How could he have changed so much—and what had happened to make him change? Morwenna's mouth trembled. It seemed Ralph Corrigan had taught his son well. And what situation existed between Matthew and April? Did he really not care —or did he mind her involvement with other men so much he had to keep up a pretence of not caring? April was stunningly beautiful—the sort of woman who would turn any man's head. Why was she flirting so openly with Phil? It could only be an attempt to gain the attention of a neglectful husband, using Phil as bait. Her brother was obviously flattered by her attention, but did it go deeper than that? Was he aware that he was being used in some kind of game between Matthew and April or had April's undoubted attractions blinded him to everything else?

Reaching the Beachcomber, Morwenna discarded her jacket and headed dispiritedly for the lounge. Aunt Jessie was there knitting, her plump body settled in the chair nearest the fire which was invariably lit in the evenings, with the approach of autumn. One or two guests lingered there, watching the oncoming sunset through the picture window, or talking idly, so any sort of personal conversation was ruled out for the time being. Only later, when the guests had retired to their rooms did Morwenna manage to convey to her aunt the gist of the conversation she'd had with Matthew Corrigan.

"So it sounds very much as if Phil's right," the older woman observed.

"I'm right about what?"

Hearing Phil's voice from the doorway, Morwenna turned. "About the plans Matthew Corrigan has for the island," she said miserably. "He wouldn't deny it to me, though I must say he didn't confirm it, either."

"Mm." Phil eyed her thoughtfully for a moment, then advanced further into the room. "We'll have to do something about it, in that case," he murmured. "Though it was only an inspired guess on my part originally. I didn't really believe he'd do it," he ended bitterly.

Morwenna eyed him silently, aware that he was thinking of the boy who had shared so many summer adventures with them.

"We must form an action group," he went on. His eyes gleamed. "We're not taking this lying down. I've already dropped hints to some of the fishermen."

"But where would he site this thing?" Aunt Jessie asked, perplexed.

"The valley down by St. Anselm's. It's the ideal spot," Morwenna responded. "I've seen Matthew down there, in fact. And he certainly seemed interested in the monks. Poor old things," she added quietly. "They will have to be moved out, of course. Life would be intolerable for them if they stayed, with a holiday complex outside their back garden."

"Strange—" Aunt Jessie looked thoughtful. "I'd always understood that the land adjoining St. Anselm's was church property; it was granted to them centuries ago, as I recall, by one of the mediaeval kings. He can't force them to move—nor can he build there without their permission. And they're not likely to grant him permission. I know times are hard, but the Church isn't that desperate for money. No, he has to have some other site in mind."

"I could find out," Phil interposed. "I've one or two—shall we say contacts? —at Corrigan Construction. It wouldn't take too long to discover just what Matthew Corrigan intends for the island—and where. Oh, by the way—" His voice became deceptively casual. "we *do* have a spare room, don't we?"

Morwenna regarded him in bewilderment. "Spare room? Well yes, but—"

"Oh it's just that April was enquiring about the possibility of staying here and I said I felt it would be all right." He smiled easily at his sister. "She'll be arriving tomorrow," he added.

Morwenna had stiffened at his words. "But why? Surely Matthew—"

"Won't worry his arrogant head one way or the other!" Phil interrupted swiftly. "The truth though, is that the cottage isn't yet habitable—not for a girl like April, at any rate. No doubt the rustic life suits him, but April is used to a more refined way of life."

"Still, I don't think it's a good idea—" Morwenna began determinedly.

"Nonsense!" Phil interrupted lightly. "Where else would she stay?" Brother and sister eyed each other.

"I'm sorry—I just don't think it's a good idea," Morwenna repeated.

"I think it's a splendid idea!" Phil returned. "What do you think, Aunt Jessie?" He smiled disarmingly at the older woman. She eyed them both thoughtfully.

"I don't see how we can refuse if Phil's already said it's all right," she murmured at last.

Morwenna flashed her an exasperated glance. Phil had always been able to twist her round his little finger! "I think it's a very bad idea," she said quietly, colour tinging her cheeks. "And I have a feeling Matthew Corrigan will think so, too."

"I don't give a damn what Matthew Corrigan thinks!" Phil said coolly.

It was useless to argue, Morwenna realised. Phil had already made up his mind that April would move into the guest house, and now he had Aunt Jessie's backing. Her eyes gleamed. Perhaps it wouldn't be for long. A girl like April would soon grow bored with Inveree—and Phil. In all probability, she would move back to the mainland soon, without too much harm being done. Closing her eyes, she wished for the umpteenth time that Matthew Corrigan had not come back to the island and things could go back to how they were before. Yawning, she stood up. Perhaps tomorrow, things would look a little better.

"I'll look in on Dad before I turn in," she informed Aunt Jessie.

"Yes. I helped him to bed a while ago," the older woman responded. "He seemed more tired than usual."

Morwenna felt a stab of guilt as she looked down at the silvery head of her aunt, bent now over her knitting.

"I'm sorry I wasn't here to help," she murmured.

Over the last few days, she seemed to have left the running of the guest house mainly in Aunt Jessie's hands. Looking up, the older woman gave her a gentle push. "Go and get some sleep," she urged, "and stop worrying so much. Everything will turn out all right in the end."

Morwenna turned towards the door, sighing. She wished she could believe that.

A light gleamed under the door of her father's bedroom as she approached it, giving rise to concern. Increasing her pace, she opened the door softly, peering into the room. The old man was out of bed, seated by the window, staring in the direction of the cliffs. Lamplight played on his face, showing up his features clearly. Blue eyes looked out of parchment skin in an unwavering stare, reminding Morwenna poignantly of the keen-eyed fisherman he had once been. Aware that he had not heard her entrance, she moved across the room, touching him lightly on the shoulder.

"Dad?"

His head jerked round and for a moment he looked at her in confusion and a certain amount of fear. Morwenna spoke soothingly to him.

"It's only me, Dad. What are you doing out of bed?"

Her eyes followed his and she saw that he had been watching Smugglers' Cottage, nestling in the shadow of the cliffs. As with the other night, a lamp burned in a downstairs room.

"He's come back." The old man's voice quivered. "See, Morwenna. He's returned to the cottage. I told him he must never come back, must stay away where they wouldn't find him."

"Shsh!" Morwenna stroked his head as

his agitation increased. "It's only Matthew —you remember I told you he was back on the island?"

"Matthew?" The old man's brow creased in a frown as if he had difficulty understanding. His gaze cleared then, focusing on Morwenna's face.

"Matthew? It's Matthew at the cottage?"

"Yes, I told you," she soothed.

He gave a deep sigh and seemed to relax. Watching him, Morwenna frowned.

"Who did you think it was, Dad?" she asked.

A closed look came over his face. "No one. Don't ask." He moved restlessly then. "I'm tired now. Help me back to bed, girl."

Slipping her arm round the frail shoulders, Morwenna guided him back to the bed. Almost immediately, the old man's eyes closed in sleep as she settled him in. Seconds later, she tiptoed out of the bedroom, closing the door quietly behind her. Her eyes were thoughtful as she made her way to her own room. Her father had obviously forgotten her telling him Matthew was back, believing the cottage to be occupied by someone else—but who? She shook her head in mystification. He was so easily confused. And since she had first told him of Matthew's arrival on Inveree, he seemed to have grown even more so.

Morwenna slept badly that night, and woke to the sound of her aunt moving about downstairs. Immediately she was out of bed, dressing herself hurriedly before heading down to help her.

"You should have called me," she rebuked, finding the older woman already halfway through breakfast preparations.

"You need your sleep," Aunt Jessie murmured. She gave her niece a piercing glance. "You've looked peaky over the last few days," she observed. "You need time off. Phil should be taking you sailing, not that woman."

Aunt Jessie's reference to April Corrigan reminded Morwenna that the woman would be moving in to the guest house that day. Unconsciously she eyed her reflection in the mirror, smoothing her hair back with an abstracted hand. The presence of Matthew's elegant wife around the place would do nothing for her morale.

She did not have long to wait for April to put in an appearance. Breakfast had hardly been cleared away before the sound of a sports car engine made Morwenna aware of the other woman's approach. She went reluctantly to the door, only to find herself forestalled by Phil, who was busily engaged in bringing in April's luggage. April's eyes rested coolly on Morwenna.

"I do hope I'm not putting you to too much trouble," she murmured.

"You're not!" Morwenna responded stiffly. Looking at Phil, she continued, "I've put Mrs. Corrigan in the small front room."

Phil's eyebrows rose at her formality but he said nothing. Morwenna turned towards the kitchen, to find her aunt's twinkling eyes on her, though she too made no comment. Later that morning, she turned to her niece.

"Now the cleaning's done, I want you to take the afternoon off," she said.

"What? There's an extra guest to cope with!" Morwenna laughed.

"I mean it." Aunt Jessie's voice was firm. "You need some relaxation. Go on

—take your sketch pad. I don't want to see you again until six o'clock."

Morwenna eyed her. When her aunt was in this mood, there was no arguing with her. Collecting her sketching materials, she left the house, heading instinctively for Lovers' Point, though she was careful to give Smugglers' Cottage a wide berth. Scrambling down to where the cliff shelved round the cove, she looked about her appreciatively. The waterfall cascaded gently down to the sea, specks of spray bouncing off rocks, polishing them until they shone in the afternoon sun. Miles of golden beach swept up to the valley, where fronds of greenery poked curious fingers in the sand. No wonder Ralph Corrigan had chosen this spot for his weekend retreat! Morwenna wondered, as she looked at the idyllic scene before her, if it might be the last year she would ever look at it in its present form. If Phil was right and Matthew Corrigan had his way, this beach would soon be filled with hordes of picnicking day trippers, outraging the locals and upsetting the monks' peaceful existence. Morwenna's mouth trembled. Would he keep the name, she wondered?

St. Anselm's Holiday Complex. Why not? He would have stolen everything else from the monks! Her eyes gleamed. Damn Matthew Corrigan! He would not be allowed to do it—not if she had anything to do with it!

The noise of a car engine alerted her and she looked upwards in its direction, to see Matthew Corrigan's car nosing its way down the cliff road. Her eyes narrowed thoughtfully as she watched it speed downwards, forking left as she had expected, towards the valley and St. Anselm's. So he was off again on his mysterious mission! Why wouldn't he admit what he was up to, face his accusers and try to justify his actions, if there was justification? On an impulse, Morwenna scrambled to her feet, her sketching forgotten. She would play Matthew Corrigan at his own game, she decided angrily. If he were not prepared to divulge his plans for Inveree, she would find them out for herself! She knew where he was headed and her intimate knowledge of the island's obscure footpaths gave her an advantage over him. Her feet skimmed the ground lightly as she threaded her way through thickets and across fields, long-forgotten haunts of her childhood. Very little had changed, evidence of the island's lack of commercialisation. Pockets of wild flowers bloomed on dry stone walls and grass verges, yet she paid little heed to them now, intent on her objective of reaching the valley in time to pick up Matthew's trail. Plunging downwards some minutes later, she sighted his car, parked some distance away from the outlying land around the main buildings of the monks' dwellings. Of Matthew there was no sign. Resuming her journey, she sped through the meadows which formed the boundary of St. Anselm's. Monks could usually be seen tending vegetable patches and other agricultural tasks. Today there was no sign of them and Morwenna guessed they would be assembled in the building for the prayer hour. But where was Matthew? And what was he up to, prowling around the place like this? Come to that, if it were indeed his intention to try and induce the monks to part with their land, why hadn't he gone through normal, legal channels instead of sneaking around, returning to the island on the pretext of getting Smugglers' Cottage ready for use again?

Aware she was nearing the outbuildings of the community, Morwenna slowed down. She dreaded to think of the monks' reaction if they found a woman on their premises. Alerted by a rustling, she stopped, her heart thudding. Then, through the undergrowth, she glimpsed the blue of an anorak and guessed she had caught up with Matthew Corrigan. She ducked, unwilling for him to become aware of her presence until she chose to reveal it. Then he stepped into full view, his back to her, keeping in the shelter of a gorse bush as he stared at the buildings before him. He was obviously making for the house, hoping to remain unobserved, presumably intent on surreptitiously entering the place. Morwenna's face flamed. How shabbily he was behaving! What did he want so much he was prepared to stoop to these methods? She could not stand and watch as Matthew, with his dubious business methods, invaded the monks' peaceful world—particularly if that world was subsequently to be turned upside down by his plans.

Stepping forward until she was only yards away from him, Morwenna spoke.

"Why don't you just go round to the front door and tell them you want them to move out?"

Matthew spun round, an expression of dismay on his face which would have been comical if Morwenna had not been so angry.

"What the hell are you doing here?"

Crossing to her, he grabbed her arm and she allowed him to draw her back into the shelter of the trees, as reluctant as he was to be discovered by the monks. Only when they were out of sight of anyone watching from the house did he face her, his eyes gleaming with an anger which matched her own.

"I'm waiting for an explanation!" he snapped.

"Explanation?" Morwenna gave a short laugh. "That sounds good, coming from you!"

"What about your methods?" he flung back at her. "Following me, spying on me. Or are you going to pretend you were just out for a walk?"

Despite her anger, Morwenna eyed him

triumphantly. It was the first time she had gained the upper hand and it was a feeling which she liked.

"No, I'm not going to tell any lies," she said calmly. "I'll leave that sort of thing to you. I told you I'd oppose you anyway I could."

"And you're not particular about your methods, are you?" Matthew said curtly.

"I have a good teacher!" she responded. Her eyes sparkled with scorn. "So what shall we do now? Go round to the front door and pay them a courtesy call?"

"I don't think they would welcome you!" Matthew growled.

"They wouldn't be particularly pleased to see you either, when I told them why you were here," Morwenna countered. "Really, Matthew!" She shook her head in mock dismay. "All this isn't necessary, just to get rid of a few old monks and take over their land, is it?" Matthew looked down at the ground for a moment.

"Would you believe me if I told you I'd no intention of doing anything of the kind?" he asked at last.

Morwenna shook her head. "I don't

think I'd believe anything you say right now," she said resolutely.

A gleam of annoyance entered his eyes. "Oh, come on, Morwenna!" His tone was impatient. "For some reason you've turned me into a monster, because I didn't tell you I was married. I didn't lie to you then. It never occurred to you to ask if I was married, did it? Most women would have wormed that information out of me within five minutes of our meeting."

"I'm not most women!" Morwenna pointed out, "And we were discussing your dubious dealings with the monks, not your matrimonial state, if you recall."

"Shush!" Matthew glanced warningly at her. "For heaven's sake, keep your voice down." He peered anxiously round in the direction of the monks' house. "Look—" he spoke patiently now, "why don't we go back to the car and talk?"

"Have you finished your business here then—whatever it was?" Morwenna asked innocently.

"Can we please move?" Matthew hissed at her.

Morwenna stood her ground. "Only

when you tell me why you were sneaking around here," she said determinedly.

"I'll tell you when we get back to the car—that's a promise!" Matthew returned.

She eyed him for a moment, then conceded, allowing him to lead her back through the undergrowth, passing through the meadow until they reached the car.

"Now—what the devil did you think you were doing, following me?" Matthew glared at her.

"I told you I'll stop you any way I can." Morwenna informed him. "I saw you heading here and decided it was time I found out for myself just what you were doing. There, I've been completely honest with you—how about you extending the same courtesy to me, as you promised?"

Their eyes caught and held, and Morwenna saw the flicker of admiration in his, before it was replaced by exasperation.

"Really, Morwenna, we're not children any more, playing games in the meadows," he said heavily.

Morwenna's eyes gleamed. "I couldn't agree with you more," she said stoutly. "So what were you doing down there?"

Matthew let out a sigh. "Okay," he said

at last. "I wanted to get a look at the monks. That's all."

"That's all?" Morwenna stared at him. "Don't insult my intelligence, Matthew! You just said we weren't children any longer. Why would a grown man want to sneak a peek at a few monks? They're just like the rest of us, except they wear sandals and long robes. Come on, you can do better than that!"

"I wanted to get a look at one of the monks," he insisted.

"Which one?" Morwenna questioned.

He ran a distracted hand through his hair. "I don't know yet," he confessed.

"Am I supposed to believe this?" Morwenna's tone was sceptical.

"I know it sounds odd," Matthew argued. "But I'm not prepared to say any more at the moment, except to give you my word it has nothing to do with a holiday complex." He spread his hands helplessly. "I ask you, Morwenna—a holiday complex! Does that sound like me? You know how I loved this island as a kid. Do you really think I'd do that to Inveree?"

"Are you saying you're not planning to

build a holiday complex?" Morwenna eyed him uncertainly now.

"I never said I was—it was you who decided that!" Matthew retorted.

"But—" Morwenna eyed him doubtfully. "Phil said—"

"I don't care what Phil said!" Matthew interrupted. His eyes gleamed with anger. "We used to be such good friends, you and I. Yet you accept without question an entirely unfounded opinion of Phil's, probably said through malice—"

"You expect him not to feel malicious towards you, when you sacked him the day after your father died?" Morwenna demanded. "You couldn't even wait until after the funeral to undo all the good things your father did!"

"Good things?" Matthew's tone was scoffing. "My father never did anything for anyone in his life without some kind of motive. Why do you think he found Phil a job in the firm? I'd have given him one willingly, but not Dad. With him, there had to be some kind of payment. As for getting rid of Phil as soon as I had the power to do so, I didn't sack him, just made it plain I'd prefer him to look elsewhere for a job. Why don't you ask him why I did that?" His voice was harsh. "Do you think April and he arrived by chance on the island at the same time? That Phil didn't know she was coming? Their affair —for that's what it is, though you may be kidding yourself it's not—began long ago, before April and I were even married."

Morwenna stared at him for some seconds. "Yet you still married her," she said at last.

He looked away. "That is not open for discussion," he said coldly. "What is, though, is what my father extracted from yours in payment. Make no mistake, Phil's job—and your art training, incidentally—were all given in gratitude for something your father had done for him."

"Art training?" Morwenna's face whitened. "That's ridiculous—my father—"

"Was a fisherman whose health had failed," Matthew interrupted crisply. "How could he find the money to send you to college—the best one around, I understand, too." Noting her stricken face, his expression softened. "I'm sorry, Morwenna. I wasn't sure if you knew or not. But I have bank receipts to prove it. I didn't tell you in order to hurt you," he added more gently, "only to show that your father had a debt to pay, like others on this island. No wonder some people call it Corrigan's Island," he added, a bitter note in his voice.

Morwenna's head was whirling. Had Ralph Corrigan paid for her art training? And, if so, why? Was he the island's benefactor, or, as Matthew had hinted, was there a more sinister motive behind his apparent acts of philanthrophy?

"If you don't believe me, come with me to your father. Ask him to tell you the truth," Matthew challenged. "In fact, we can kill two birds with one stone. I need to talk to your father. I believe he helped my father in a particular way—and I have to know what it was. I already suspect most of it but there are things only he can confirm."

"What things?" Morwenna looked at him helplessly. "What are you talking about?"

"I can't say yet," Matthew shook his head. "But I'll tell you the reason for my interest in the monks. Whilst sorting out my father's affairs after his death, I came across something rather curious. According to his financial records, he had been making regular donations over a number of years to the monks here—covenants, I believe they're called."

"So? Your father helped a lot of people on this island," Morwenna pointed out. "And many business men make donations to charitable institutions."

"Not religious institutions—not if you're an atheist as he was!" Matthew insisted. "And not in a separate personal bank account. There had to be a payment for services rendered; I knew him better than you did. Those monks earned their donations and I think your father can tell me just how they did it."

"If what you say is true, why don't you just ask them?" Morwenna responded.

"Because I don't want to spook them until I'm certain of my facts." Matthew looked at her impatiently. "And only your father can confirm them."

Morwenna frowned. Something more wide-reaching and strange than she could have imagined was unfolding here. There was something else niggling her, too.

"Why didn't you deny it when I first accused you of wanting to build a holiday complex here?" she asked.

Matthew had the grace to look embarrassed. "It suited me to let you go on thinking that, since you'd already decided that was my intention," he admitted. "It gave me a cover for my real reason for being here. And now that you've forced me to confide in you, I'll have to ask you to keep all this to yourself until I know the rest of the story and can fit the missing pieces into what I already know."

"Then you'll tell me?" Morwenna asked.

Matthew's face sobered. "You—and the whole island—will know all about it, you can be sure of that," he said harshly.

His words chilled her. What had happened all those years ago, involving their respective fathers?

"I have to talk to your father, Morwenna." Matthew urged. "I'll be as gentle in my questioning as possible, believe me. I have the highest regard for your father. Will you let me speak to him? If you refuse, I'll respect that. But I'll go on searching until I find the truth."

He would, too, Morwenna thought, eyeing him silently. He would chip away, bit by bit, until the events of the past—which he was so certain had taken place—were uncovered. Her brow furrowed. Perhaps it would be better for her father to unburden his secrets—if he had any, so that they no longer tormented him. His last days should be peaceful, free from fear of things done in the past.

"Let me see how he is today," she conceded at last. "But if he doesn't want to talk to you—"

"Trust me, Morwenna." Matthew gripped her hand. "This time, trust me."

She looked up at him, seeing for the first time since his return to the island a glimpse of the boy she had known long ago—a boy who would never have harmed her family or the island.

Some time later, Matthew's car drew up outside the Beachcomber. As she alighted, Morwenna's eyes flickered to the window of her father's bedroom. What secrets had he kept to himself all these years—things which tormented him even more, now that Matthew had returned? Falling into step beside him, she walked towards the door, stopping as it opened to reveal Aunt Jessie.

"Thank heavens you're back!" The older woman's usually calm voice was high with fear.

"What is it—what's wrong?" Morwenna grabbed her aunt's arm in concern. Struggling to gain control of herself, the older woman looked into Morwenna's eyes.

"It's your father," she said unsteadily. "I took a drink up to his room, only to find he wasn't there." Her voice trembled. "He's not in the house at all, Morwenna. He's gone and we can't find him anywhere."

4

"GONE?" Keeping her voice steady, Morwenna looked at her aunt in bewilderment. "What do you mean—gone? Have you checked the bathroom—"

"I've looked everywhere, searched the garden, even!" Aunt Jessie cut in. "He just isn't in the house at all, Morwenna."

Morwenna felt the colour drain from her face. It couldn't be possible for him to have left the house under his own steam; he was too ill, too fragile to move far at all without help. She became aware of Matthew's hand on her arm, steadying her.

"He can't have gone far." He spoke reassuringly. "He hasn't had much of a start." His voice sharpened. "Where's Phil?"

Aunt Jessie regarded him helplessly.

"Out sailing, I think, with April."

"Of course—he would be!" Matthew made an impatient gesture. "Is he ever around when you two need him? Never mind—" he went on quickly as Aunt Jessie began to protest. He took command of the situation. "If you can see to things here with the guests, Morwenna and I will deal with this." He touched her arm reassuringly. "We'll find him in no time, Aunt Jessie. You mustn't worry. Now where's the likeliest place he'd head for?"

The older woman's face crumpled. "I'm afraid for him," she whispered.

Despite her own shock, Morwenna responded swiftly. Taking her aunt's arm, she piloted her back into the house and sat her down on a chair.

"It will be all right," she said then with a conviction she didn't feel. "Matthew and I will find him. You see to the evening meal for the guests. Get Mary up from the village to help for an hour. Can you do that?"

The older woman made an effort to pull herself together, nodding.

"Good." Morwenna smiled encouragingly at her, before turning to where Matthew was waiting. Without speaking, they both ran back to the car parked by the kerb and in seconds were moving away.

"Where to, first?" Matthew looked at her enquiringly.

"Oh, I don't know." She made a vague movement with her hand. Even now it seemed incredible to her that her father had managed to leave the house unaided, let alone get this far away. She clenched her fists in an effort to control the sudden fear which threatened to overwhelm her.

"It's my fault," she said unsteadily then. "I shouldn't have left Aunt Jessie alone for so long. Dad's been disturbed over the last few days—"

"Stop blaming yourself!" Matthew's voice was terse as he interrupted her. "It won't do any good. You said he seemed disturbed. Did he say anything which might give us a clue as to where he'd be likely to head for?"

Morwenna forced herself to think back calmly. "I found him out of bed last night when I looked in on him," she recalled. "He was sitting by the window, watching your cottage."

Matthew's hands tightened on the steering wheel.

"The cottage?" His voice filled with suppressed excitement. "So. It all comes back to the cottage, doesn't it? We'll try that road first."

Accelerating, he swung the car to the left, heading in the direction of the cliffs. Beside him, Morwenna sat in numbed silence, her eyes straining in an effort to catch a glimpse of her father's shambling figure. Her mind raced ahead fearfully, conjuring up horrific visions of him lying injured—dead, even—by the side of the road. She closed her eyes as tears, hot and prickly, came into them. Her father was her responsibility and it was because of her neglect that he was missing now. He was the reason she had come back to the island in the first place and if anything happened to him now through her carelessness, she would find it hard to forgive herself. Her shoulders slackened. Covering her face with her hands, she felt the wetness of her tears on her palms.

"Stop it, Morwenna!" Matthew's voice was rough. "There's no time for that and it won't solve anything. Keep an eye on the road—" his voice tensed suddenly. "What's that over there—look!"

Tears forgotten, Morwenna stared in the direction of his pointing finger. She could make out a dark shape by the side of the road which led to a clearing, her eyes straining to identify it.

"It *is* him!" Matthew's voice was grimly triumphant as he increased speed. As they drew near, Morwenna saw that it was indeed a human being, half lying on the ground, and she let out a gasp of mingled relief and fear. She was out of the car almost before Matthew had stopped, running heedlessly across the gravelled road towards the spot where Tom Wainwright lay. The frail head turned at her approach and she saw that his eyes were open.

"Dad—" Reaching his side, she crouched down, gathering the frail figure into her arms and holding it to her. The old man's bony frame quivered in her arms and for a moment Morwenna allowed the tears of relief to fall unheeded down her face, on to his shoulders. Then Matthew was beside her, prising the old man gently away from her.

"Help me get him into the car," he instructed.

Despite the hardness of his voice, his movements were gentle as he gathered the old man into his arms and lifted him up. Rising with him, her eyes never leaving her father's face, Morwenna helped them slowly towards the open door of the car. Her father's face was a ghastly colour and though he was conscious, it was plain that he was in a state of complete exhaustion, his skin waxen and cold to the touch, his limbs flopping uselessly.

Despite the old man's frailness, it was obviously taking Matthew all his time to carry him and Morwenna watched anxiously, afraid he would stumble. Neither of them spoke until the old man had been lowered with infinite care into the back seat, where he lay full length. Scrambling in beside him, Morwenna raised his head, laying it tenderly in her lap. She was hardly aware now of Matthew's presence, her attention focused fully on her father. His eyes closed now, his breathing was rapidly becoming laboured, as she watched over him. What had made him do this crazy thing? What had been his intention when he began this hopeless journey? He must have known there was no possibility of his getting far. Why had he done it? Morwenna could hardly begin to understand his reasons, yet she was sure of one thing. They were mixed up in some way with Smugglers' Cottage and the reasons why Matthew Corrigan had returned to the island. Tom Wainwright had been disturbed by thoughts of the cottage for some days now and it looked as if he had been trying to make his way there. What lay behind the old man's erratic behaviour? What was he so afraid of? Morwenna's eyes gleamed. When this was over and her father safely back in his bed, she would insist on knowing everything, she vowed savagely. The time for hints and evasions was over. She would demand that Matthew tell her the whole story; her father's well-being was all that mattered, and it could not be guaranteed until she knew everything.

Matthew drove at a steady pace back to the Beachcomber, darting anxious looks over his shoulder at intervals. At last they were drawing up outside the guest house and he slowed the car.

"Go round the side, if you can!" Morwenna urged. "We may be able to get him into the house without attracting the attention of the guests."

Nodding, Matthew turned the car to the left, stopping outside the kitchen door. It opened immediately, to reveal Aunt Jessie's plump figure. Running towards the car, her eyes darted anxiously to them.

"It's all right, we found him!" Morwenna soothed. "He's okay—exhausted, but that's all, I think."

Wrenching open the rear door, Aunt Jessie peered inside, her eyes on the old man's face. Then Matthew was gently drawing her away, leaning inside to gather the old man into his arms, with Morwenna's assistance. With difficulty they levered him through the kitchen door and inside the house. The clatter of dishes and guests' chatter could be heard from the dining room, yet Morwenna was hardly aware of them. Her eyes never left her father's face as she helped Matthew carry him upstairs. It took some time, and they were both breathing heavily by the time they reached the old man's bedroom. Hovering anxiously beside them, Aunt Jessie opened the door, then stood aside to let them enter. Laying the old man's inert figure down on the bed, Matthew stood back, eyeing him soberly.

"Should we call the doctor?" The older woman looked automatically to him for guidance.

"I think that would be a good idea," he responded. She left the room. Morwenna sat down, feeling suddenly weak and close to tears again. Closing her eyes, she leaned against the chair back.

"Why did he do such a silly thing?" she whispered. Turning, Matthew walked across to the window and stared out, across the cliffs.

"The answer lies there!" he said quietly, nodding in the direction of Smugglers' Cottage. "That's where it all began. And where, I think, it will all end."

Opening her eyes, Morwenna stared at him. "What's it all about, Matthew?" she asked unsteadily. "I have to know now. We're all involved."

Matthew moved restlessly. "This isn't the time," he murmured. "Wait until your father is settled."

"Oh no, you don't!" Morwenna's voice became stronger and she eyed him defiantly. "I want to know what's going on —now!"

Her voice rose on the last word and Matthew looked round at her quickly. Aware of his scrutiny, Morwenna fought to control her rising hysteria, which was, she realised, a reaction to the trauma of the last hour.

"Pull yourself together, Morwenna—" Matthew broke off, and she heard his quick, indrawn breath. Looking up, she saw that he was staring past her, towards the bureau by the side of her father's bed.

"That carving—" Matthew's voice was suddenly urgent. "Where did you get it?"

Frowning in bewilderment, Morwenna followed his gaze to a carving of a deer standing on top of the bureau. His eyes gleaming, Matthew crossed the room in quick strides and picked up the carving, turning it round and round in his hands, whilst Morwenna watched in mystification.

"Where did you get this?" His voice tense, Matthew repeated the question.

Morwenna shook her head helplessly. "I think one of the monks did it for Dad a long time ago," she said. Her eyes widened as the implication of her own words hit her. The monks of St. Anselm's again . . . Standing up, she crossed to where Matthew stood, looking at the carving over his shoulder. Its graceful lines were perfectly executed on the smoothly polished wood. Wordlessly, she stared at Matthew. His face illumined with excitement, he continued to turn the carving over and over in his hands for a few moments longer.

"What's so important about it, Matthew?" she asked at last, unable to bear the suspense any longer.

"What's so important about it?" Matthew's eyes blazed suddenly. "It proves what I suspected, that's all!"

"How?" Morwenna eyed him in mounting frustration. "Honestly Matthew, you're talking in riddles! You've never even seen this carving before!"

"No, but I've seen one identical to it," he informed her grimly.

"And where is this other one?" Morwenna asked.

"In my office at the factory," he said tersely. "The office which used to be my father's, in fact."

"So what does that prove?" Morwenna asked.

"I'm certain that the carvings were done by the same man." Matthew's voice was thoughtful. "And if so, it's one more piece of the jigsaw slotted in. Tell me, Morwenna—" he eyed her speculatively. "What would my father be doing with a carving done by one of the monks of St. Anselm's?"

"They do sell crafts," Morwenna pointed out. "He might even have bought the thing from us; we do stock their work in the showcase in reception, as you noticed when you came here the first time."

"No."

At the sound of Aunt Jessie's voice, they both turned to see her in the doorway. Eyeing them thoughtfully, she crossed the room, looking anxiously at the sleeping man on the bed before turning to Matthew and taking the carving from him.

"We stock wines and homemade sweets, if you recall, Morwenna—their main lines of work. This carving—" she tapped it with her finger, "this is one of only a few done by one of the monks. It's his hobby, and the things he makes are never offered for sale."

Matthew's eyes flared with triumph as he heard her. "This monk—tell me about him," he murmured.

"He's known as Brother Stephen," the older woman said, eyeing Matthew in puzzlement. "He's very old; almost a recluse."

"Yes, I'll bet!" Matthew muttered.

Morwenna and her aunt exchanged mystified glances.

"And how long has this Brother Stephen been at St. Anselm's?" Matthew asked.

"Oh—" Aunt Jessie hesitated. "I'm not sure. All I do know is that he's old and keeps to his cell a lot. Strange thing about him, though—"

"Yes?" Matthew questioned.

She frowned. "Well, he's sick and he always wears his hood pulled round his face, to hide a disfigurement, I understand."

"Disfigurement?" Matthew's voice was taut with excitement. "A burn, perhaps?"

Morwenna's eyes rounded as she realised where the conversation was leading. There was a fire at Smugglers' Cottage some years ago . . .

"What are you getting at, Matthew?" she asked. "What does all this mean?" Matthew looked at her, his eyes gleaming.

"It means, if my suspicions are correct, that the monk you know as Brother Stephen isn't really a monk at all."

"Who is he, then?" Morwenna's voice held an agony of suspense. About to reply, Matthew turned, listening, as voices sounded outside. The door opened and Phil entered, followed by an older man carrying a medical bag.

"Doctor North! Thank heavens!" Aunt Jessie started forward.

"Now then, don't distress yourself, Jessie!"

The doctor touched her arm reassuringly, before making his way to the figure on the bed. Quickly he took the old man's pulse.

"What happened?" he asked, a minute or two later.

"That's what I'd like to know!" Phil's voice was curt.

Morwenna hastened to explain. "Apparently he wandered out of the house without anyone seeing him," she began. "We found him—Matthew and I, that is—on the cliff road. He was in a state of collapse."

"Cliff road?" Doctor North shook his head in wonderment. "What on earth was he doing there? I wouldn't have thought it within his capabilities. Has he done this before?"

"It's the first time, to my knowledge!" Morwenna responded. She hesitated. "He's seemed a bit agitated this week; excitement, I suppose." She gestured vaguely. "Phil coming back—and Matthew."

"Mm—"

Doctor North was examining the old man quickly and expertly as she spoke. Stirring, Tom Wainwright opened his eyes, gazed uncomprehendingly at the doctor, then closed them again.

"I don't think he's any the worse for his adventure, barring understandable exhaustion," the doctor declared eventually, straightening up. He spoke in a louder voice then to the old man. "Now then, Tom! What have you been doing, tiring yourself out like this?"

The old man stirred and they heard his quavering voice.

"Mustn't find out . . ."

Morwenna's face tensed at his words. "That's what he was saying before," she said. "He seems obsessed by Smugglers' Cottage."

"Oh?" The doctor eyed her questioningly. "Any reason for that?"

"Perhaps we should ask the owner of the place," Phil suggested.

Noting the way Phil and Matthew eyed each other, Morwenna moved hastily to intervene.

"I think we should discuss this later," she said. "Once Dad is settled." She looked at the doctor. "If there's no real harm done, we should get him to bed now."

Picking up his bag, the doctor nodded. "I'll look in again tomorrow. Meanwhile, I'll leave some sedatives for you to administer to him in the evenings. You shouldn't have any more trouble with him wandering again."

"Thank you, Doctor." Morwenna looked at him gratefully. It would be a load off her mind to know that her father was sleeping peacefully at night.

Between them, she and Aunt Jessie made the old man as comfortable as they could, once the men had left the room. Morwenna's mind was filled with questions as she worked. What was it Matthew had started to tell them about the monk known as Brother Stephen? She could hardly wait to rejoin him and hear the rest of the story. Pausing, she became aware then of men's raised voices. Shaking her head, Aunt Jessie looked across at her.

"Go down to them, Morwenna. Sounds like those two are tearing into each other and they'll be upsetting all the guests. I'll finish off here."

Morwenna needed no second bidding. The last thing she wanted was a confrontation between her brother and Matthew Corrigan. Things were bad enough . . . Speeding down the stairs, she frowned as the men's voices grew nearer. They were in the kitchen and she headed in that direction immediately.

Matthew and Phil were facing each other, their faces tight with anger, confirming her fears. Swiftly she closed the door behind her, before eyeing the two men in mounting anger.

"Haven't we had enough for one day, without you two flying at each other's throats?" she demanded.

Matthew seemed more in control than Phil did, she noted, without surprise. Phil always had been the hot-headed one.

"You're right, of course. I'd better leave," Matthew said stiffly.

"I haven't finished yet!" Phil's tone was savage. "Just why was my father trying to get to your cottage?" His voice strengthened. "Ever since you came back, there's been trouble of one kind or another."

"Oh?" Matthew's eyebrows lifted expressively. "Seems to me there hasn't been half as much trouble as there should have been." His mouth twisted. "After all, it's not every man who'd take no action whilst his one-time best friend's fooling around with his wife."

"Fooling around?" Phil's voice was suddenly icy. "Is that what you think it is?"

"Oh dear." Matthew shook his head in

mock dismay. "Don't tell me you think you're in love with her?"

"What if I am?" Phil grated. "It would serve you right to lose her—and that's what's going to happen. She's leaving you for me."

"Oh, come on!" Matthew's voice was openly mocking now. "If you think that, you don't know April half as well as you think you do! She likes the good life and social position too much to leave me. She's using you, Phil—and you're an idiot if you can't see that."

Phil breathed jerkily. "She loves me," he said in a low voice.

"She doesn't love anyone except herself," Matthew interrupted crisply. "When you get to know her a little better, you'll find that out for yourself!"

Morwenna listened to them, appalled. How had they come to this, these two who had once been such great friends?

"Please—" she said unsteadily. "Keep your voices down. And try to control yourselves. Dad's had enough for one day."

Phil's face worked. "Tell that to him! He's the cause of it all!" he said violently, before turning on his heel and walking out of the room.

Morwenna regarded Matthew helplessly. Never one to enjoy unpleasantness, she'd had more than her share of such scenes today. All she wanted now was peace and quiet, time to think; mull over the events of the last few hours. Picking up his coat, Matthew left the room, Morwenna staring silently after him. Only when he had been gone for several minutes did she remember that he had not explained how the carving in her father's bedroom tied in with the reason he was on Inveree. She was no nearer to learning what it was all about, apart from the fact that there was a definite connection between all the events which had occurred over the last few days.

Guests were leaving the dining room now, talking cheerfully among themselves. It was plain they had heard nothing of the evening's drama. Only April still lingered over coffee when Morwenna went into the dining room to help Mary, the girl from the village, clear away the dishes. Coolly, April watched as Morwenna busied herself, keeping her face averted from her. She was in no mood for exchanging pleasantries, her mind filled with the events of the last few hours. She longed to know what Matthew had been about to tell them before Aunt Jessie interrupted them earlier and was angry with herself for allowing him to leave without further explanation. She would have to call on him tomorrow, though the thought hardly appealed to her, recalling his set face as he left. A thought struck her then.

"Mrs. Corrigan—" She turned hesitantly towards the other woman still watching her lazily through narrowed eyes.

She was looking particularly beautiful that evening in a low-cut dress of jade silk, which set off her blonde colouring perfectly. Morwenna, hot and untidy from the efforts of the last few hours and with no time to even think about her appearance, put an instinctive hand to her hair, brushing it back from her eyes.

"Oh dear," April regarded her in mock apprehension. "I hope you're not about to ask me to help with the dishes?"

"Of course not!" Morwenna flushed with embarrassment. "I was just wondering—that is, I need to speak urgently to Matthew. I know he had a telephone installed at the cottage."

"That's Matthew!" April pulled a face. "Business is never very far from his mind." She regarded Morwenna steadily. "Have you found out what he's up to yet on the island? I suppose it *is* a holiday complex?"

About to correct her, Morwenna changed her mind suddenly. Instinctively she decided to say nothing to April of Matthew's real reason for being on Inveree, particularly as she knew so little of it herself. If Matthew had wanted his wife to know, he would have told her himself. And so far, the other woman had given Morwenna no good reason to trust her with any confidences. April was regarding her speculatively now.

"You wanted to speak to Matthew?" she pursued.

"Yes. I don't have the number; he left in rather a hurry . . ."

"Oh, so it *was* his car I saw drawing up earlier," April murmured. "Did you have a pleasant day out?" she went on, her eyes wide with innocence.

Morwenna flushed. "It wasn't exactly an

outing," she said hurriedly. "I bumped into him whilst I was out sketching, and he gave me a lift home."

"Please!" April looked at her in pretended horror. "You don't have to explain to me! Matthew is free to do as he pleases—though I ought to warn you, it can't lead anywhere."

Morwenna's colour had heightened at her words. "I think you're misunderstanding the situation!" she said stiffly. "Matthew and I are old friends from childhood, that's all."

"Oh yes, he told me." April eyed Morwenna reflectively. "The little sister."

Something about the way in which she said it drew Morwenna's anger. "There's nothing between Matthew and me!" she retorted. "Your modern ideas on marriage don't extend to us."

Realising she had gone too far in her anger, Morwenna stopped, expecting an angry retort from the other woman. To her surprise, however, April threw back her head and laughed.

"Oh, you're so quaint!" she said mockingly at last.

Eyes gleaming, Morwenna resisted the

urge to slap the hard, beautiful face so near her own.

"And you're wrong, you know," April went on, sobering.

"About what?" Morwenna found it difficult to speak politely.

"About there being nothing between you and Matthew," April informed her. She eyed Morwenna thoughtfully for a second. "He's not exactly indifferent to you," she said then. "As for you, you don't even realise you're in love with him, do you? I knew it, the first time I saw you." She shrugged. "It was obvious that he hadn't told you about me, though you carried it off well, I'll give you that. It was naughty of him, but then—" her eyes sparkled. "that would have spoiled the fun, wouldn't it?"

Morwenna could no longer conceal her acute dislike of April. Who would have thought anyone so beautiful could at the same time be so horrible? And—it wasn't the first time Morwenna had asked herself this question—what had Matthew Corrigan seen in her? He was no fool. Surely her obvious beauty couldn't have blinded him to her equally obvious faults?

Stacking plates on top of each other, Morwenna picked them up. The sooner she was out of the room the better, she thought savagely, whilst she could still trust herself not to do something she would regret.

"Don't you want the number?"

April was smiling at her now, clearly amused by her discomfiture. She was the sort of woman, Morwenna thought angrily, who would thrive on the harm she caused. There was something very twisted in her character, and it was becoming more apparent every day. Yet she did want Matthew's telephone number badly.

"If you don't mind giving it to me," she forced herself to reply. Opening her handbag, April produced a piece of paper on which she scribbled rapidly.

"Here." She handed it to Morwenna. "Give him my love when you call him!" she added impudently.

Ignoring her last remark, Morwenna took the paper and gathered up the pile of crockery, before leaving the room. Twin spots of colour tinged her cheeks as she headed for the kitchen. At the sight of her aunt, she stopped.

"Dad—is he—" she began.

"Sleeping soundly," the older woman said reassuringly. "I think we can relax a little now, Morwenna. He's been lucky. What, I wonder, made him do such a silly thing?" Anxiety creased her homely features. "You don't think he'll make a habit of it, do you?"

"Of course not," Morwenna soothed. "Doctor North said the tablets should settle him down at night. During the day, we'll just have to keep a closer watch on him, that's all." She looked at her aunt contritely. "I'm sorry I wasn't here earlier to help. I meant to be back hours before but I had what can only be described as a skirmish with Matthew Corrigan."

"I'm glad you did!" Aunt Jessie's tone was vehement. "What would we have done without him? What I don't understand is why your father was heading for Smugglers' Cottage in the first place. He knows it's no longer his responsibility and hasn't been for a long time. Why would he try to go there, after all this time?"

"I think perhaps I may be able to throw some light on that the next time I talk to Matthew Corrigan," Morwenna murmured. "There's something going on which I don't understand." She changed the subject, eyeing the older woman hesitantly. "Aunt Jessie—Matthew Corrigan told me today his father paid for my art training. Do you know anything about that?"

Aunt Jessie's back was turned, so Morwenna was unable to see her face. For a moment she didn't reply. "He wanted you to have your chance," she said at last. "There wasn't much money coming from the guest house and his fishing days were long over."

"So it *is* true!" Morwenna eyed her shrewdly. "I would have thought my father too proud to accept that kind of help from anyone."

"Ralph Corrigan wasn't just anyone!" Aunt Jessie responded. "It's nothing to be ashamed of, Morwenna. Your father did enough for the Corrigan family and there are more people than him on this island who have cause to be grateful to Ralph Corrigan."

Listening to her, Morwenna felt a flicker of apprehension. Matthew had used almost the identical words, but he'd gone further, inferring a sinister motive. She shook her head despondently. When would she know the truth behind the puzzling facts which were slowly emerging? She eyed her aunt tentatively again.

"This monk—Brother Stephen, you said?—you've obviously seen him, to be able to describe him."

"Only a glimpse through a window," Aunt Jessie told her. "He was pointed out to me by one of the other brothers when I asked about the man who did the carving. It seems he wanted your father to have it as a gift in gratitude for something, though I never found out why. Anyway, he was whittling at some wood even then, sat in the garden all alone. He doesn't exactly welcome strangers—not that any of the monks are all that sociable."

"And you've never spoken to him?" Morwenna asked.

Aunt Jessie shook her head. "Why all this fuss about one monk?" she wanted to know.

Morwenna sighed. "Don't ask me," she muttered. But first thing in the morning, she vowed—she would be asking Matthew.

Later, Morwenna retired to bed, utterly exhausted by the excitement of the evening. Peeping into her father's bedroom, she satisfied herself that he was still sound asleep, then made her way to her own room. Phil had not come back and she guessed he would not return until his anger had cooled. April, too, had slipped out of the guest house, and she wondered if they had a prior arrangement to meet. Not that it mattered. She would, she realised, be glad when Phil went back to the mainland. His visit had brought none of the usual pleasure this time; they had seemed to spend most of their time bickering.

Blue skies and misty sunshine held the promise of another beautiful day, when she awoke the following morning. She felt rested and more relaxed than she had the previous evening. Hurrying to her father's room, she was reassured by his even breathing and the return of slight colour to his cheeks. With luck, he would be none the worse for his adventure.

"Wenny!" Phil's voice was curt as he walked into the dining room some time later.

"Oh, it's you, Phil. Do you want some breakfast?" Morwenna forced a cheerful note into her voice, aware that her brother's mood was still uncertain.

"No." He shook his head. "Did you manage to find out anything at all about why Corrigan's here?" he asked bluntly then.

Morwenna eyed him sharply. First April—now Phil. "He did give me his word that it wasn't anything to do with a holiday complex!" she said carefully. "And we weren't exactly on confiding terms."

"How did he come to be with you yesterday?" Phil demanded. Morwenna coloured.

"I—I bumped into him whilst I was out," she explained, "and he gave me a lift home. Aunt Jessie met us with the news of Dad's disappearance when we arrived and we set out immediately in search of him."

"How is he this morning?" Phil asked.

Morwenna felt irritation. It ought to have been a natural thing for him to pop into his father's bedroom on his way downstairs and see for himself how he was. He'd made such a fuss yesterday—or was that more to do with Matthew being here, she wondered now?

"He's calmer," she informed him. "And looking better for a good night's sleep."

"Good." Phil frowned. "So we're no wiser about why Corrigan's here. I spoke to my contact at Corrigan Construction last night, after I left here. He knows nothing of any plans to build on Inveree—and he would be the one to know, if there was anything planned."

Morwenna felt a great weight lifted from her, at Phil's words. So Matthew had been telling the truth yesterday. Aware of her changed expression, Phil eyed her thoughtfully.

"Watch your step with that man," he cautioned. "I know you've a soft spot for him. He's not your sort, Morwenna."

Her irritation increased. "Apparently his wife is *your* sort!" she countered acidly.

Phil flushed. "Let's not get into that subject," he muttered.

"I couldn't agree more!" Morwenna retorted. "Though I can't help warning you to watch *your* step! Those two are using you."

Phil scowled. "You've been listening to Matthew Corrigan too much," he grated. "Isn't it just possible April might have some genuine feelings for me?"

Morwenna felt a sense of foreboding as she listened to him. Though older than her by several years, he seemed at times child-like and naïve. And, despite what he seemed to have convinced himself of, she was certain that Matthew Corrigan's assessment of his wife was more accurate than Phil's.

"Anyway I aim to find out what he's up to," Phil was saying now.

Morwenna attempted reasoning. "Could be he's here for exactly what he says he is—to open up Smugglers' Cottage for visiting."

"Why didn't he come before, if that's the case?" Phil demanded.

"Because he was probably too busy, what with school and university, then learning the business . . ." She broke off. Why was she making excuses for Matthew Corrigan?

"Well, I intend to go over there and find out," Phil threatened.

"Oh no!" Morwenna looked at him in

horror. The last thing she wanted was a repetition of the previous evening's events. "Look—" she touched his arm cajolingly. "I'm ringing Matthew later; there's something I want to clarify with him. Let me try to find out, gently."

Phil looked undecided. "Okay—see what you can worm out of him," he said at last. "I'll talk to you later."

Morwenna sighed with relief as he strode out of the room.

The hallway was deserted when she dialled the cottage's number some time later. Her heart seemed to beat quicker as she waited. It was picked up almost immediately and she heard Matthew's unmistakable tones over the line..

"Matthew? It's me, Morwenna!" she said hesitantly.

"Morwenna?" He sounded surprised. "I was about to ring and enquire after your father."

"He's a lot better, thank you!" she responded.

There was an awkward pause and she knew Matthew was waiting for her to give him her reason for ringing.

"Matthew, I have to talk to you," she

said at last. "That business with the carving last night; you left things rather in the air."

"I haven't really anything concrete to tell you." Matthew's voice was guarded. "I intend going over to St. Anselm's after lunch."

"May I come with you?" Morwenna couldn't hide her eagerness.

There was a momentary silence. "Actually, I was wondering—" he hesitated, then continued. "if I could borrow the carving in your father's bedroom? It may come in handy to identify the man who made it."

"Certainly. I'll bring it over if you like," Morwenna volunteered.

"There's no need—I'll collect it from you," Matthew said.

"It's no trouble!" Morwenna said determinedly. If she arrived at the cottage with the carving, he could hardly drive off to St. Anselm's and leave her there.

"Okay." He sounded reluctant. "I'll see you later."

Putting down the receiver, Morwenna turned to find April Corrigan eyeing her with amusement from the doorway. Colour flooded into Morwenna's cheeks. Had April heard her conversation and realised she was speaking to Matthew? By the look in her eyes, she had. Turning, Morwenna hurried away towards the kitchen. Another exchange with April was not something she would welcome.

It was late morning when she set out for Smugglers' Cottage. Having satisfied herself that her father was still sleeping soundly and informed her aunt of her intention, she slipped out, heading towards the cliff road. The sun was high in the sky now, bathing everything in its glow. Morwenna's eyes were appreciative as she hurried along. The view, now that the early morning mist had lifted, was superb. The sea was calm and inviting, the cliffs forming a jagged backdrop to the beach which swept round the coastline on this side of the island. Smugglers' Cottage, picturesque and rambling, came into view, bringing sudden, poignant memories of childhood with it. Morwenna's eyes softened. They had been so carefree then, the three of them, secure in their friendship, despite their differing social classes.

Now, they seemed worlds apart and that friendship seemed to count for nothing.

The door of the cottage was ajar when she reached it and no one answered her timid knock. Going round the back of the cottage, she heard the sound of the rushing waterfall, and stood for a moment to admire the view from Lovers' Point. She frowned. Where was Matthew? He hadn't left without her; his car was still outside the cottage. A sudden sound caught her ears; at the same time she saw April's car pull in to the side of the house, out of sight of the main cliff road. Then she was looking further, to where the sound came from, some yards from the car. A couple were locked in a close embrace, and as Morwenna stared at them, she realised it was Matthew and April.

5

"YOU realise of course that little scene was engineered especially for your benefit?" Matthew's voice was sardonic.

Looking away from him, Morwenna settled herself into the passenger seat of the car. "It really has nothing to do with me," she said stiffly.

Yet the angry flush on her face belied her words. Coming upon Matthew and April embracing like that had been a shock, after the conclusions she had drawn about their marriage. Now she realised what a fool she was. Infidelity came easily to people such as they. Not content with keeping her brother Phil on a string, April was apparently keeping her options open in respect of her marriage. How lightly they played with other people's feelings, she thought now. And, she acknowledged, it wasn't only Phil's feelings which concerned her, but her own.

As she had stared at them minutes ago,

they had become aware of her presence. Immediately, Matthew had tried to break away from his wife but her arms entwined round his neck, had held him close to her for a moment longer. She had turned then, following Matthew's gaze, an amused laugh coming from her as she saw Morwenna watching them.

"Oh dear!" Her voice had carried clearly to Morwenna's ears. "We've been discovered, Matthew darling."

With an angry movement, Matthew had succeeded in disentangling himself from her, striding across to where Morwenna stood, without another glance at his wife. One look at his set face had told Morwenna he was extremely angry—though whether it was directed at April or herself, she wasn't sure. Nor did she care, at that particular moment. What kind of game were these two playing, she wondered now? Didn't it matter to them who got hurt in the process? She recalled Phil's words spoken in anger to Matthew the previous evening, yet none the less sincere for that. His feelings, it had been obvious, had gone beyond mere flattery at April's attentions; he was in love with her, and she must have known that. Yet it seemed she took his affection as lightly as she apparently took Matthew's. Morwenna had been surprised, too, by the depths of her own feelings, coming upon that scene the way she had. Now she pulled herself up sharply. She had been allowing her feelings towards Matthew Corrigan to develop in a direction they should never have taken. Seeing April in Matthew's arms was the jolt she needed to bring her to her senses. She tried to analyse her own feelings objectively as she waited for Matthew to start the car. Of course she felt a certain attraction for him; what woman wouldn't? He was good looking, successful and knew what he wanted. But that was as far as it went—or should be. Her eyes smouldered. *And would be*.

"She must have seen you coming up the road," Matthew spoke suddenly, his voice careless, with just a trace of amusement. His anger, she noted, had cooled. "And so I found myself suddenly treated to an overly display of wifely affection. For which, I suppose, I ought to thank you." Hearing the mockery in his voice, Morwenna shrugged.

"There's no need to explain. I'm only sorry I intruded on such a tender scene," she said sweetly. She had been unable to resist the jibe and was rewarded by the flush which spread over Matthew's face. "Here—" she thrust the bag she was carrying in his direction. "The carving you needed."

Settling herself back in her seat, she stared out of the window. What he had said could be true, she realised. April had overheard her telephone conversation with Matthew earlier and would have known she was on her way. But by the same token, Matthew also knew she was about to arrive at the cottage. Her mouth tightened.

"I think I can hear the telephone ringing." Matthew was looking in the direction of the cottage. There was indeed a faint ringing to be heard. "I'm popular this morning, wouldn't you say?" he murmured drily, opening the car door. "I'd better see what it is; it might be something urgent." Seconds later, he was back, his face serious. When he spoke, there was no trace of his earlier mockery in his voice.

"That was your Aunt Jessie," he told

Morwenna. "It seems your father's . . ." he hesitated, "taken a turn for the worse."

"Dad?" Morwenna looked at him in alarm.

"In the circumstances, I'd better postpone my trip to St. Anselm's and get you back home!" Matthew said swiftly.

Later, Morwenna hardly remembered anything of the journey back to the Beachcomber. All she was aware of was the need to get back to her father's side, and her own condemnation of herself for having left him. It must be urgent, for Aunt Jessie to telephone the way she had. Matthew glanced in her direction several times, yet no words were spoken until they reached the guest house. Morwenna's heart sank as she saw Doctor North's car drawn up outside the guest house. Almost before Matthew had stopped the car, she was out, running up the path into the house, to be met by a grim faced Phil. Some instinct told her she was too late. Helplessly she searched her brother's face, hoping desperately that her instincts were wrong, but the slight shake of his head only served to confirm them.

"It must have been in his sleep," he said

huskily, as she clung to him. "So peaceful, Morwenna. Remember that."

"No! No!" The cry was wrung from her.

Burying her head against his chest she wept, Phil holding her tightly until her sobs had subsided a little. At last she made an effort to pull herself together.

"I shouldn't have left him . . ." Her voice was incoherent.

"You knew it was expected," Phil said gently.

"Aunt Jessie. I must go to her," she murmured unsteadily then.

"She's with him," Phil murmured.

Turning, Morwenna headed for the stairs. As she did so, Matthew, who had been waiting quietly in the background, touched her arm.

"Morwenna—"

She looked at him in surprise for a moment, having completely forgotten his presence.

"I'm sorry," he said quietly.

Nodding, she moved away from him to go to her father.

The old man looked so peaceful he might still have been asleep. Wonderingly, she touched the cold cheek with her fingers, as if to convince herself he really had gone. Seated by the bed, Aunt Jessie seemed calm as she held his hand.

"No more pain for him, Morwenna!" she said softly. Waves of grief washed over Morwenna. "I shouldn't have left him!" she said wildly, "I should have taken greater care—"

"It would have happened." Doctor North spoke gently from the back of the room. "Perhaps it's best this way, my dear, rather than a lingering, painful end."

Crouched by the side of the bed, Morwenna wept as if her heart would break. She knew the doctor meant well, but for the moment, his words brought no comfort.

The next few days passed in a flurry of activity leaving, thankfully, little time to think. Funeral arrangements kept Morwenna fully occupied, in addition to the running of the guest house. The last remaining guest—apart from April Corrigan—was due to leave that weekend and by mutual consent, Morwenna and Aunt Jessie decided not to take any further guests for the foreseeable future. The season was almost over and neither woman had the heart for the social courtesies demanded by having people in the house. Once the first sharp anguish had passed, Morwenna was able to see more clearly that her father's death had been inevitable, and in many ways a blessing in disguise, as the doctor had said. Still she tormented herself, feeling she had not taken seriously enough the agitation which had led to his leaving the house and exhausting his already diminished strength, undoubtedly accelerating his death. And if only she had looked more closely at him that morning, before setting out for Smugglers' Cottage! It seemed to her then that she had been allowing her judgment to be clouded by Matthew Corrigan's return to Inveree, so that she pursued small mysterious happenings, rather than the real issues of her life.

The morning of the funeral was particularly difficult to get through. Phil, serious and unusually formal in dark suit, hardly spoke to anyone. Aunt Jessie, calm and dignified despite red rimmed eyes, seemed to grow frailer by the minute. Morwenna herself was shattered, yet knew she must bear up for the sake of the others. She had not seen Matthew since the day of her father's death, though she noted his presence at the family funeral. The church was crowded with villagers paying their respects. Fishermen who had served with her father in the past formed an unofficial guard of honour, grave faced and uncomfortable in unaccustomed collars and ties. Morwenna's eyes were blinded by tears when she saw them. Her father, she knew, had been held in high regard by the island community and now they had gathered to make their final farewells. One man in particular, Wyn Roberts, whom she remembered from childhood as one of her father's shipmates, touched her arm briefly at the end of the service. Old now, he sailed alone, keeping himself apart from the rest of the islanders, and she recalled the local belief that he was "touched". Yet the blue eyes which gazed unflinchingly into hers were clear enough.

"A finer man never sailed," he said quietly now.

Nodding her thanks, Morwenna turned away, unable to control her grief in the face of his simple words.

The house was quiet when they returned from the churchyard. Opening the shuttered window, Morwenna felt as if her father's spirit soared away as the sunlight flooded into the room. Tears stung her eyes again at the thought. Leaning against the window, she closed her eyes, thinking of the frail old man who had left them so recently.

"Morwenna."

At the sound of Matthew's voice, she turned to see him hovering uncertainly in the doorway. Pulling herself together, she made an effort at politeness. It seemed years since she had sat in the car outside Smugglers' Cottage. Such things seemed trivial now, beside the overwhelming grief of her father's death. Advancing further into the room, Matthew eyed her.

"You mustn't feel bad about not being around when your father died," he said quietly, "or because he managed to get out of the house the day before."

"Nevetherless—" Morwenna tried to speak calmly. "I should have taken better care of him."

"No one could have taken better care of him than you and your aunt." Matthew's voice was compelling. Coming to stand beside her, he took her arm, forcing her to look into his eyes. "You mustn't blame yourself." He made a vague movement with his hand. "If only I hadn't come back; he wouldn't have tried to get to the cottage . . ." His voice trailed away.

"Now who's blaming himself?" Morwenna murmured.

He nodded. "As you can see, we all have a share of blame, if there is any. He was a very sick man, Morwenna, and he died in his sleep, without pain. For that at least, you have to be thankful."

Morwenna turned away, unable to reply. Some day, she knew Matthew's words would be the consolation he intended them to be. For now, all she could feel was grief, mingled with guilt.

"Have you been to St. Anselm's yet?" Forcing a change in the conversation, she looked questioningly at him.

He hesitated. "I decided to wait. I . . ."

She looked at him quickly, realising with surprise that he too was grief-stricken at her father's death. They had, she recalled, been close, many years ago.

"I would like to have paid my respects to him," he murmured now.

She touched his arm. "You did that this morning," she told him.

"Anyway—" His voice became brisker. "I decided to leave my visit to St. Anselm's for a day or two, particularly as you'd said you wanted to come, too." He hesitated. "I planned to go later today, in fact—but if you'd prefer to leave it—"

Morwenna eyed him in surprise. She hadn't expected such consideration. And now, more than ever, she wanted to know the truth of what happened at Smugglers' Cottage long ago. It would keep her mind occupied, she realised. Months of caring for her father had left a gap in her life which she needed to fill, and though her curiosity at Matthew's reasons for being on Inveree had receded over the last few days, now they came back with increased vigour.

"I should stay with Aunt Jessie," she said hesitantly.

"One or two of the village women are planning to sit with her this evening; I heard them arranging it," Matthew informed her.

Morwenna made up her mind. "Then I'm coming with you," she said.

It was some time after seven when Matthew returned for her.

"You still want to come?" he asked, as she met him at the door.

"The sooner it's done, the better!" she responded. There was a flicker of something she couldn't immediately identify in his eyes for an instant as he regarded her, then without another word he turned and left the house, Morwenna at his heels.

Moments later, they were settling themselves inside the car. Stealing a glance at him, she saw that Matthew's face was impassive as he eased the car forward and headed it towards the road which led to the valley.

Was he, like her, anticipating the events at the end of the journey, she wondered? Her heart seemed to beat against her ribs. In the space of a few short days, her life had been turned upside down. Was it only the other day she had been standing in her room, bemoaning her fate and the prospect of this dull existence continuing indefinitely, dividing her time between nursing her father and helping Aunt Jessie run the

Beachcomber? Now, a myriad of unanswered questions tormented her. Would this visit answer them, ending the frustration she had felt—or was Matthew over-optimistic?

Almost as if reading her thoughts, he spoke. "Before long, I should have the answers to all the questions I've been asking myself, ever since Dad died!" he murmured.

"Thank heaven for that," Morwenna responded.

They were within sight of the valley now, the building in which the monks of St. Anselm's lived a shape looming up out of the evening gloom. In spite of herself, Morwenna eyed it with apprehension. What secrets lurked within its walls, waiting to be told? Who was the mysterious Brother Stephen, if as Matthew had hinted, he wasn't a monk? She longed for Matthew to explain, yet, eyeing his set profile, she asked no further questions.

Pulling up outside the gatehouse, Matthew left the car, covering the ground in quick strides, Morwenna close behind him. As he rapped the door knocker, the noise resounded eerily to Morwenna's taut nerves, "What's the head man's name?" Matthew asked urgently, as shuffling footsteps sounded from within.

"Oh—" Morwenna cast around in her mind. "Brother Dorian, I think," she whispered.

At the sound of bolts being drawn back, she moved instinctively, edging herself behind Matthew. With much creaking, the door swung open, to reveal one of the monks, an elderly man with a hesitant air about him.

"Hello!" Hardly waiting for him to speak, Matthew addressed him. "I'm sorry to disturb you at this hour. My name's Matthew Corrigan. I must speak to the person in charge—Brother Dorian?—urgently."

The monk regarded him curiously. "It *is* late," he was beginning, before Matthew interrupted him.

"I know, and I wouldn't intrude if it were not important," he said quickly. "Please, just a few words with your superior."

The monk's eyes fell on Morwenna and he frowned.

"Perhaps we could wait somewhere

away from your community," Matthew suggested quickly, aware of his disapproval.

Nodding, the monk opened the door just wide enough for them to step inside.

"There's a waiting room here—" he indicated a door to the left. "If you'd care to make yourselves comfortable . . ."

"Thank you."

Matthew cast a glance over his shoulder at Morwenna, his eyes gleaming with satisfaction. Clearly, he had half expected the monk to turn them away. Morwenna glanced curiously around as they entered the small waiting room. Dank, with a musty air about it, the only light came from a small window high in the wall, though there was an oil lamp on the table, which the monk lit before leaving them. The light played on them, bringing their faces into sharp relief. Matthew's features were taut with anticipation. Leaning forward, he tapped impatiently against the wall with his fingers, as Morwenna watched him. He hardly seemed aware of her presence, at that moment. This was the culmination of weeks of speculation, Morwenna realised. Would he, once he had found what he was looking for, revert to some semblance of the boy she had known—or was that Matthew lost for ever? This man beside her was in many ways a stranger, yet it seemed they had shared so much over the last few days that he was, for now, like someone she had known all her life. Would they, once this was over, go their separate ways again, or . . . Morwenna's face shadowed. He has a wife, she reminded herself sharply. No matter what the situation is between him and April, Matthew is a married man.

Carried away by her thoughts, she hadn't realised that the monk had returned, this time accompanied by another, taller man. The newcomer had an authoritative air about him which distinguished him quickly from his subordinate.

"Brother Dorian?" Matthew was on his feet immediately, holding out his hand. "My name's Matthew Corrigan—"

"Yes. So I am informed. Welcome."

Brother Dorian regarded Matthew thoughtfully. It occurred to Morwenna then that he did not seem particularly surprised to see him.

"This is Morwenna Wainwright, whose aunt you may know from the Beachcomber Guest House." Matthew was introducing her.

"Welcome."

The monk inclined his head in Morwenna's direction, then turned back to Matthew.

"How can we help you?" he asked.

Without hesitation, Matthew plunged in. "I'd be obliged if you'd allow me to speak to one of your brothers—Brother Stephen, I believe he's known as."

The last part of the sentence, with its scepticism, was not lost on the monk. He and Matthew eyed each other steadily. Watching them, Morwenna felt the rising flow of excitement within her as she speculated on whether the man had any idea of why they were here, Whatever the truth of all this, she thought, he can't fail to be aware of some of it.

"I'm afraid our brothers are not permitted visitors," Brother Dorian said at last.

"Oh?" Matthew's eyebrows rose expressively. "Then perhaps you would be kind enough to answer some questions regarding him yourself—such as how long he has been here? Where did he come from? What's his real name?"

"Why do you want to know these things?" Brother Dorian asked.

Matthew's gaze did not waver from the other man's face. "Because I believe he may be a relative of mine," he said at last. "Someone whom I'd long thought dead."

There was a silence between the two men, broken at last by Matthew.

"I don't mean him any harm," he insisted. "But I have to speak to him. If you refuse permission for me to do that, I will have to enlist the help of others."

The implication of official involvement had the desired effect.

"Brother Stephen came to us seeking sanctuary within our community," Brother Dorian told them reluctantly. "Whatever —whoever—he was before he came is of no account. He is now Brother Stephen and I have a duty to protect him from those who might bring harm to him."

"I told you, I'm not here to harm him!" Matthew protested, "but I have to know what happened the night he came here. Only he can tell me."

The two men eyed each other for a long moment. At last the monk nodded.

"I will ask Brother Stephen if he will see you," he said, turning to leave the room.

Matthew's eyes blazed with triumph. Left alone, he and Morwenna waited in tense silence. Turning after a moment, he eyed her questioningly.

"Do you believe this Brother Dorian knows nothing about all this?" he asked.

Morwenna frowned. "If he says he doesn't—" she was beginning, when he interruped her.

"Why would he accept money from my father all this time if he didn't know it was a bribe to keep quiet about something?"

Morwenna sighed, as she heard him. "You don't know much about your fellow humans, Matthew," she murmured. "Or maybe you're so used to the dubious ethics of the business world, you can't recognise simple goodness any more."

Matthew looked sceptical. "At its best, it's naïvety these people have shown. At worst, they helped in a cover up."

"Cover up?" Morwenna's voice was sharp. "Is this Brother Stephen a criminal then, Matthew? You told Brother Dorian he was a relative. Isn't that true?"

"Yes. If he's who I think he is, he is indeed a relative," Matthew informed her quietly.

"Who is he?" Unable to bear the suspense any longer, Morwenna looked at him beseechingly. "For heaven's sake, Matthew, who is he?"

So intent was she on Matthew she hadn't noticed the door had opened again to re-admit Brother Dorian. Immediately behind him was another man, a small, shambling figure with stooped shoulders. His hood was drawn up closely round his face, his hands concealed in the voluminous robe he wore. Nowhere was there any indication of his identity. Matthew rose slowly to his feet, his eyes on the newcomer. Remaining seated, Morwenna watched the proceedings silently. The atmosphere, already tense, had become even more charged, and no one seemed willing to break the silence. At last Matthew took a tentative step forward.

"Uncle Stefan?" he murmured hesitantly.

For a moment the man didn't answer,

then his hand came up to draw back the hood slightly from his face, enabling him to see Matthew clearly. Watching, Morwenna had a glimpse of faded blue eyes and the beginnings of a livid patch on the man's right cheek. The only sign he gave of any emotion was the sudden trembling of the gnarled hand holding the hood away from his face.

"You are Nadia's son," he said at last.

His voice had a marked accent and his whole demeanour was that of a very old man—yet from what she could see of his face, Morwenna judged him to be only in his sixties. Involuntarily, her heart went out to him. Whatever had caused such suffering, she wondered? He was like a leaf blown over in the wind, buffeted by stronger forces. Whatever he had done in the past or whatever had been done to him, should not have returned to haunt him now, she thought impulsively. Matthew, too, seemed to be having difficulty in controlling his emotions. Stepping forward, he clutched the monk's hand and for a moment they embraced each other silently. Watching them, Morwenna felt her eyes blurring with sudden tears. So it had not just been the desire to get to the bottom of a mystery, on Matthew's part! He had genuinely wanted to trace the man because he was a member of his own family. Morwenna felt certain then that Matthew would do nothing to harm this frail old man, now he had found him. Brother Dorian and Morwenna herself seemed at that moment to be onlookers, no longer part of the scene being played out before their eyes. Indeed, she felt an intruder on something intensely personal and private.

At last the old man broke away from Matthew.

"My sister—she is well?" His voice was anxious as he questioned Matthew.

"She's well!" Matthew reassured him swiftly.

Turning, he looked at Morwenna. "As you've heard, this is my Uncle Stefan," he said in a husky voice. Brother Dorian moved restlessly, speaking for the first time since he had returned with Brother Stephen. "I think we had better sit down," he murmured. "There is much to be told here, I think."

Brother Stephen moved to obey him and

the tension in the atmosphere lessened somewhat as the men seated themselves again. Matthew spoke first.

"You may not know, Morwenna, that I am only half English. My mother is Hungarian; my father met her on a business trip many years ago. After a brief courtship, they married, though it was only with difficulty that Mother was allowed to come to this country to be with my father. I knew all about Uncle Stefan —my mother's only brother. He and my mother exchanged letters for many years and it was her dearest wish that he be allowed to join her in Britain. Then the letters stopped and I was told he was dead." He looked across at the old man. "As you see, he is very much alive!" he ended softly.

The old monk took up the story, speaking hesitantly at first, then as the tale proceeded, his voice became stronger.

"I worked for many years on merchant ships sailing all over the world," he explained. "I received letters regularly from my sister in Britain. She told me of her family, and of this beautiful island where they had a cottage. I pictured it all in my mind—and I longed to be with her. After my wife died, I was alone in the world, my parents having been dead for years. I began to think more and more of Nadia, my cherished little sister who had left us so long ago to go to her husband's country. I longed to see her again. I was afraid to let the authorities know of my wishes, feeling it would not have been permitted. Yet there was another way." His eyes gleamed. "I bided my time until the ship on which I worked travelled to Britain. Then I slipped away from her in the darkness. I knew from Nadia's letters the location of the island and the existence of the hidden path which ran from the beach up through the cliffs to the cottage. She had described it all so vividly in her letters. Somehow, I found my way here, though I knew people from the ship would have been sent after me once my absence had been noted." He shuddered for a moment. Watching him, Morwenna felt a surge of compassion. "I managed to reach the island and the cottage. I stayed there for a while, hoping that sooner or later someone from the family would come. Yet when I was discovered, it was not by one of the family, but by a stranger."

"That would be your father, Morwenna!" Matthew put in swiftly. "He kept an eye on the place when we weren't there," he informed the monks.

"Yes. My friend, Tom!" Brother Stephen agreed. Morwenna and Matthew exchanged glances and she saw the warning written clearly in his eyes. *Don't tell him. It won't do any good now.*

After a moment, the old man continued. "Of course, he was going to inform the police of my presence at first, not knowing who I was. I spoke very bad English then. I had in my possession a letter from my sister and I showed it to him. It had, of course, your address at the top, Matthew, and Tom realised there was some connection. Soon afterwards, your father came to the cottage, Tom having contacted him. At first he did not know what to do about me." The old man shrugged whimsically. "I had entered the country illegally and there was no certainty your Government would grant me asylum. If they had sent me back . . ." Again, he shuddered.

"What about the fire—who was the man who died in it?" Matthew asked.

A shadow crossed the old man's face.

"Your father left me at the cottage for a few days, until he had decided what to do. I looked forward to his promise to bring my sister to see me. But before that could happen, something else occurred. The man who had been pursuing me from the ship managed to catch up with me. He arrived at the cottage late at night, determined to take me back. There was an argument, followed by a violent struggle, during which a lamp was overturned, which started the fire. I had been knocked to the ground and lay there dazed for a while. When I awoke, the fire had spread." His voice trembled and he turned beseeching eyes to them. "I tried to save him, Matthew—I swear that to you, but the fire had taken hold quickly and I was beaten back by the flames. I knew I had to get out immediately or I would be killed myself. So I had to leave him to his fate." There was anguish in his voice and instinctively Morwenna reached out and clutched his hand.

"It wasn't your fault!" she said urgently.

He looked at her sorrowfully. "But it was, my dear. Because of me, he died." His voice was gentle. "Since then I have prayed constantly for his soul and in reparation for my own sins." He bowed his head for a moment, then went on with the story. "Of course, no one except Tom and my brother-in-law knew there had been anyone at the cottage. I managed to drag myself clear of the blaze, though I was severely burned." He touched his partly concealed face for a moment. "The shock must have affected my memory. For some weeks I was completely unable to recall the events of that night. I had managed to crawl into a cave where I lay for several days. Instinct must have led me to Tom's cottage then. Of course, I was too confused to see the implications, at that stage. I found out later that the body in the cottage was assumed to be that of a wanderer—" he waved a vague hand in the air.

"Tramp?" Matthew supplied quickly, and Stefan nodded.

"You can imagine Tom's reaction when

he saw me, having thought I was the one who'd died in the cottage. I needed medical help and he did not know what to do with me. At last, he brought me to the monks here at St. Anselm's. They took me in, ministered to me—and I have been with them ever since," he ended simply.

After he had finished speaking, silence hung on the air for several seconds.

"And they never came looking for you again—or the other man?" Morwenna ventured at last.

The old man shrugged. "I have been safe here. Who knows, for years I may have been dead to them. As for the other man—" he shook his head, leaving the sentence unfinished.

"And my father—he must have been told you'd survived the fire," Matthew eyed him shrewdly. "Presumably he decided it was better all round if things were left the way they were. I know he made regular donations to your community," he added, looking at Brother Dorian. That man inclined his head.

"For which we were grateful," he responded, "though it would have made no difference. Brother Stephen was welcome here. I knew, of course, there was some connection between them, though I have not heard the whole story until now. So far as we at St. Anselm's were concerned, Brother Stephen was a man who needed our help. And later, when he had recovered and chose to join our community, we were overjoyed."

A look passed between the two monks and again Morwenna found a lump in her throat. "So you really are a monk," she murmured.

"Yes." Stefan smiled. "This is the only life I want. And now that I know my dear sister is well, my heart is full." Leaning forward, he tapped Matthew's arm and smiled into his eyes. "You are so like her, So . . ." he made an eloquent gesture with his hands. "Hungarian!"

"It's good to meet you at last, too!" Matthew said. "Presumably my mother doesn't know you're here?"

"I think not," Stefan murmured. "Your father came to see me. He told me that he had been about to break the news to Nadia that I was here, yet before he could do so, there was the fire. You must remember for several days he would have thought I had died in the fire." A shadow crossed his face. "It seemed then the easiest way out of the difficult situation was to let things remain as they were. Your father did not think your Government would allow me to stay and if my own countrymen thought I was the man in the fire, they would have stopped looking for me."

"And of course it would have enabled him to close the book on what would have been, for a man in his position, a potentially embarrassing situation." Matthew's voice was dry. His eyes became thoughtful. "And there may have been another reason why he would prefer my mother not to know her brother was still alive. But—" His expression suddenly became closed. "That's another story."

Morwenna frowned. So there was more to be told? Yet, eyeing his suddenly grim face, she had a feeling he was not going to be forthcoming about it.

"What led you here?" Brother Dorian eyed him curiously now. "After all this time, how did you come to know about Brother Stephen?"

"There were several things," Matthew admitted. "It wasn't until recently that I heard the story of Uncle Stefan's defection—but, like the person who told the story to me, I believed he had died in the fire. Then I found out about my father's contributions to your community and I began to wonder why. He was not of your faith, Brother Dorian—or indeed, of any faith. I was beginning to suspect Uncle Stefan might still be alive, when I saw the carving in Morwenna's father's bedroom." Delving into the bag on the seat beside him, he produced it and held it out to the other man. "A carving which exactly matched one in my father's office and obviously done by the same man."

"Ah!" Stefan's voice was wry. "So my self indulgence, my desire to give something—the only thing I had—to those who helped me in my time of need, was my undoing."

"The carvings are beautifully done," Matthew told him sincerely. "My father treasured his; it had pride of place in his office. He was asked many times who created it, but he never told anyone including me—and, I assume, my mother."

"Your mother was the reason he helped

me," Stefan reflected. "At first he was going to inform the authorities, as of course he should have done. But he wanted so much to unite us; the little sister I had not seen for years, his beloved wife —and the man from nowhere." He spoke lightly but there was an underlying pain in his voice.

Eyeing him, Morwenna saw the glint of tears in his eyes. "Perhaps soon . . ."

"Perhaps." The old man agreed.

Matthew stared at them silently.

"What will you do now?" It was Brother Dorian who broke the heavy silence which had settled on them all. "Will you make this known to the authorities—" He eyed Matthew searchingly. "Or will you allow your uncle to go on living in peace here with us at St. Anselm's?"

"Of course there's no question of Brother Stephen being disturbed!" Morwenna said quickly, before Matthew could reply.

Matthew rose to his feet. "I think it's time we left for the moment," he said quietly. "It's late and it's been an emotional meeting. But, if permitted, I'd like to see my uncle again when convenient." He looked questioningly at Brother Dorian, who nodded.

"Our house is yours," he said quietly.

"And of course there's no question of my father's contributions to your community stopping," Matthew affirmed. Leaning forward, he clasped his uncle's hand for a moment. "It's good to have met you at last, Uncle Stefan!" he told him.

"And you, my nephew." The old man's voice quivered slightly.

Turning, Matthew made to leave, Morwenna following. In seconds they were being let out of the building by the monk who had first admitted them. Stepping outside into the cold evening air, they were both silent as they made their way to the car. As she climbed in, Morwenna turned and gave the shuttered building a backward glance. What incredible things it sheltered within its walls! Shivering, she turned to Matthew.

"So the story's told at last," she murmured. "No wonder my father became disturbed when you arrived on the island. He must have carried the secret of your Uncle Stefan around with him for years, dreading its discovery. And, once your father was dead, he would be the only one left in possession of the knowledge."

"That's where you're wrong, Morwenna!" About to start the car, Matthew spoke unexpectedly. "Other people did know about it. How do you think I found out about Uncle Stefan's defection in the first place? My father certainly wouldn't have told me! And because of those others, there's only one way out of this."

Eyeing him, Morwenna was aware of a feeling of dismay growing inside her. "Which people? Who else knew, Matthew?" Her voice sharpened. "And what do you mean—one way out of this? There's only one possible course of action and that is to do nothing. Your uncle has paid for his wrongdoing—if a desire to see his sister and escape a cruel regime can be construed as wrongdoing."

"I'm sorry, Morwenna." Matthew's voice was determined. "But I can't agree with you. Uncle Stefan must come out into the open—declare himself to the authorities."

"You can't be serious!" Morwenna

regarded him in horror. "They'll send him back—he'll be killed—"

"They'll let him stay, once they've heard his story, I'm sure of it!" Matthew insisted grimly. "But it must be done, Morwenna—and I'll have to see that it is done!"

6

MORWENNA stared disbelievingly at Matthew. Was this the same man she had watched only minutes ago, embracing the uncle he had not even known was alive until recently? Could he really be intending to expose the shambling old man who had hidden himself from the world, after a lifetime of harsh endurance? He had not, she recalled, answered Brother Dorian's question when that man had asked him what he intended to do now.

"I don't believe I'm hearing this," she said at last.

Matthew kept his eyes on the road. "I understand how you feel," he said after a moment. "But believe me Morwenna, I don't intend my uncle any harm."

"You don't intend him any harm?" Morwenna eyed him incredulously. "When you're about to throw him back into the spotlight where he faces the possibility of being packed off back to his own country, not to mention alerting the men who were pursuing him when he arrived in the first place? Are you serious, Matthew?"

"Morwenna—" There was brusqueness now in Matthew's voice. "The men who were pursuing him all that time ago now believe him to be dead. In any case, they couldn't do anything to him now. All he has to do is explain what happened and apply for permission to stay. When all is said and done, he is an illegal immigrant!"

"He's your uncle, for heaven's sake!" Morwenna exclaimed, eyeing him in exasperation. "What's wrong with you, Matthew?" she challenged then. "You can't get on with your family. You hated your father because he was a successful business man; you're prepared to see your mother's brother sent back to possible death even though he's never done you any harm—"

"I never made any secret of my feelings about my father, nor the reason why I felt that way!" Matthew interrupted. "Do you really think the way he acted in this business was the best, in the circumstances? Who benefited from it—my mother?" He made a savage gesture. "She doesn't even know her brother's still alive, let alone that he's been in this country for so long. Or Stefan? Shut away in a monks' community for the rest of his life—"

"He seems more than happy to be there!" Morwenna cut in spiritedly. "Don't try to justify your actions, Matthew! You're about to disrupt an old. man's life, possibly even have him imprisoned—all for your own selfish ends. Or is it to satisfy some ridiculous code of honour you may have?" Her voice rose. "You despised your father but his code of honour outshines yours any day."

Matthew's face had flushed a dull red. "It wasn't honour that made my father help Stefan," he said quickly, "he would have turned him in without a thought if it hadn't been for my mother. She was my father's blind spot, the only weakness he had. It was because of her he didn't hand Stefan over to the authorities straight away, once he learned of his presence on the island. He knew only too well how my mother longed to see her brother again. How do you think she would have reacted if he'd turned Stefan in? It would have been in all the papers; Stefan sent back to his own country to face the music. There's no doubt my mother would have turned against my father—and he knew it. He was devoted to her, I'll say that for him!" His voice strengthened. "No, Morwenna, I'm afraid it wasn't a misplaced sense of duty which made my father act the way he did." Scorn had crept into his voice. "If he'd really been doing it from the goodness of his heart, he would have tied up all the loose ends instead of laying himself—and me—open to blackmail, the way he did."

"Blackmail?" Morwenna's eyes rounded as she heard him. "What do you mean by that?"

Matthew hesitated. "I hadn't meant to bring all this into it," he muttered. "Though now you know about Uncle Stefan, it was inevitable you'd have to know the rest eventually. Quite apart from the fact that my father ought to have severed his financial connection with the monastic community or at least concealed it well enough for it not to be traced, there was also the question of keeping the knowledge of Stefan's presence on the island restricted to as few people as possible; people he was certain he could trust. Your father, of course, was drawn into it unwittingly, and my father never doubted his loyalty in any case. But there was another person who, by accident or design, was let in on the secret; his chauffeur, Sam Ingram. April's father," he added quietly.

Morwenna waited, saying nothing. She had a feeling that the reason for the unconventional relationship between Matthew and his wife was about to be disclosed at last.

"When your father contacted mine after finding Stefan at the cottage," Matthew continued, "he came over here straight away, his chauffeur driving him. He was unable to drive himself at the time; some sort of injury to his arm, I believe—and somehow or other, Sam Ingram got wind of what was happening. Whether my father confided in him, being a trusted employee of many years, or whether he nosed it out for himself, I'm not sure. April wasn't too forthcoming on that point. All I do know is that he retired shortly after that with a more than generous pension."

"April?" Morwenna echoed. "She knows about your uncle then?"

"Oh yes." Matthew's tone was bitter. "All this I learned from April shortly after my father died. It wouldn't have been so bad if Sam Ingram had kept his mouth shut, but he didn't, apparently. He was a widower, and his only child—April—was still at school. He must have passed the information on to her; either that, or she wormed it out of him in that endearing way she has." His mouth tightened. "Sam Ingram had a heart condition," he continued quietly. "Shortly after retiring, he died. My father took his daughter into our home, to be brought up as a member of the family—a role she enjoyed to the full." His voice hardened. "The best finishing school, foreign holidays, introduction to the cream of society; in fact, everything she wanted, he gave her. And she revelled in it. Of course, everyone assumed it was out of loyalty to his old employee that my father had his orphaned child brought into our home, but, knowing him as I did, I often wondered what was the true reason. As I've told you before, my father never did anything for anyone unless there was something in it for himself. I found out just what that something was as soon as he died, when the price of April's silence was transferred to my account. Only, by that time, the price had gone up."

Listening to his revelations, Morwenna could hardly believe what she was hearing. "Are you saying she blackmailed you into marrying her?" She could not keep the incredulity out of her voice.

"That's exactly what I'm saying!" Matthew responded. "She'd been making her intentions obvious for a while, though I'd managed to hold her firmly at arms' length. Then she came and told me the real reason for my father's taking her into the house—with marriage her price for keeping silent."

Morwenna looked away from him, her mind trying to absorb what he had just told her. "It's incredible," she said at last.

"Nevertheless, it's true!" Matthew told her grimly. "April did very well out of our family; the life style suited her. And, once I'd inherited the firm, being my wife would make her position doubly secure. What could I do?" He spread his hands in a gesture of defeat. "Even though both she and her father believed Stefan to have been the man who died in the fire, the knowledge of what had happened could still have harmed my family, not to mention people who had worked for us for years. The part my father played in the affair could have led to criminal conviction, had he still been alive. Once he was dead, that danger was removed, but there was still your father's involvement to be taken into account. I don't know what the penalty is for aiding an illegal immigrant. Besides that, there was the distress it would have caused my mother if things had been brought out into the open. That's the one thing my father and I had in common, Morwenna. We both adore her." His tone was bitter. "So what could I do?" he finished quietly, "apart from accepting April's terms?"

"So why has it changed?" Morwenna eyed him challengingly. "Why are you now prepared to harm our fathers' memories, not to mention hurting your mother and exposing your uncle to possible deportation to his own country? And the monks; they would be in trouble for harbouring him no matter how they protested they didn't know the whole story."

"I've told you." Matthew's voice was stubborn. "Stefan's been here for so long they're bound to look sympathetically at his case."

"You think so?" Morwenna's voice was sceptical. "And open the door for every seaman disenchanted with his own country to defect as soon as the ship hits port? If you think that, you're naïve, Matthew—and I'd never have called you that. No—if you want to open the whole subject, it's for reasons of your own!"

"I want Stefan to be in this country legally and free to spend his life with my mother!" Matthew insisted. "It would bring her a lot of happiness to have him near her."

"Why can't you just bring her quietly down to visit him?" Morwenna demanded. "I doubt if your uncle would want to come out into the world anyway now. He has taken his vows, after all."

"I can't bring her here for the same reasons I think my father didn't tell her Stefan was alive," Matthew said patiently.

"Because April was still living in the house. If my mother starts making sudden visits to the monks, it wouldn't take April long to figure out the reason why. She's no fool. Perhaps my father was waiting, expecting April to marry and leave us—" his tone was bitter. "Of course, he didn't realise she would contrive to marry herself into the family. Which means, that as long as April lives, the threat hangs over us and my mother can never know that her brother is alive and living in this country. I can never divorce April and I doubt if she'll ever leave me—unless she meets someone she thinks is a better proposition than I am. And I'm afraid your brother hardly comes into that category." There was a savagery in his voice which shocked Morwenna, listening. "Which should make it clear to you that he, like me, is just one of April's toys," he added.

Morwenna shuddered. She had disliked April Corrigan on sight, the woman's self centred, calculative nature soon becoming obvious, yet never in her wildest dreams had she realised the extent to which that woman's ruthlessness stretched.

"I'd never have imagined that in this

day and age a woman could force someone into marrying her." She looked helplessly at Matthew. "Why? With her looks and the social position being part of your family gave her, she could have had almost any man she wanted. Why did she have to choose someone who so obviously couldn't stand her?"

"Probably for that reason!" Matthew's tone was wry. "It would be a challenge for someone like April, to try and make me fall under her spell, like all the others. There have been a lot of them, both before and after we were married. Your brother isn't the only one to enjoy her favours!"

Morwenna looked away, at the mention of Phil's involvement with Matthew's wife. A man like Phil, she saw now, would be like putty in April's hands, just another plaything with which to taunt Matthew.

"He has to know," she murmured. "Maybe then he'll see what he's getting into and stay away from her."

"I doubt it!" Matthew said heavily. "She has him caught hook, line and sinker —and he's hardly likely to believe it anyway. He'll think it's just a ploy to alienate him from her. Not only that, but it would be downright dangerous to let him in on this. He could let something slip to April, alerting her to the fact that Stefan is still alive. And who knows then what would happen? We only have Stefan's word that the other man died accidentally in the fire."

"But she'll know anyway if what you plan for Stefan happens!" Morwenna pointed out, "or have you changed your mind?"

"No." Matthew dashed her hopes immediately. "But I want it done properly. It's the only way. Stefan must make a clean breast of things." He drew a hand across his face eyeing Morwenna helplessly. "I *have* to believe they'll let him stay, Morwenna—can't you see that? I can't live under April's blackmail for the rest of my life; being made a fool of, having her dangling her conquests under my nose! Maybe I could have gone on, but not now."

"Why not now?" Morwenna touched his arm urgently.

For a moment he didn't reply, then, turning he looked into her eyes. "Before it didn't matter," he said quietly. "I could have put up with her behaviour for my mother's sake." His face shadowed. "At some point in the future, when my mother was no longer here . . ." his voice trailed away for a moment. "I could have taken steps to remove April from my life, without too much harm being done to the firm. It wouldn't have mattered."

"It would have mattered to my father," Morwenna murmured.

Matthew nodded. "He would have had to be kept out of it somehow," he agreed. "He was, after all, acting under my father's instructions."

"My father was a free man!" Morwenna said quickly. "What he did, he would do out of loyalty to your father but not because he was bound by him. And he would have felt compassion for your uncle, too, wanting to help him."

"Unlike my father!" Matthew muttered. "It must have seemed like the answer to a prayer when his uninvited guest appeared to have been burned to death in that fire at the cottage."

"Was the fire the reason you never came back to the island?" Morwenna eyed him shrewdly.

"Partly," he admitted. "But mainly it was because of April. I didn't want her anywhere near Inveree. I knew my friendship with you and Phil would be threatened, once she became a part of our group. As it is, I was wasting my time," he added quietly. "Phil and I will never be friends again, by the look of it. But there was another reason for not coming. After the fire, my father had the place cleared up, but discouraged us from using it. Looking back, I wonder now if he wanted to keep it as a contingency plan—another hiding place for Stefan, if he decided at some point to leave the monks."

Morwenna stirred restlessly. The revelations of the last few minutes had shocked her, leaving her mind grappling futilely with the facts which had emerged, and their implications. For a moment she wished that her original interpretation of Matthew's return—a holiday complex—had been the correct one. How simple that sounded now! Something they could have fought, out in the open. Not this hole in the corner business—again she shuddered. April, far from being a bored, spoilt wife looking for excitement, was in fact a ruthless adversary playing a dangerous game with calculated shrewdness. Only now did Morwenna understand the extent of Matthew's difficulties; the things which had changed him for ever from the idealistic boy for whom she had felt such friendship. He was caught in a web of deceit spun long ago, its far-reaching effects clouding his life and the lives of those around him. And could she blame him for trying to escape if he saw a way out—even at the expense of other people's happiness? His father was dead—hers, too. Only their memories could be hurt. But there was his mother and Stefan—and, it seemed, he was prepared to sacrifice their happiness for his own. She became aware then that Matthew was speaking again, his voice low.

"If I hadn't found you again . . ." He hesitated, then looked deep into her eyes. "If I hadn't found someone I could love, if I were free . . ."

"No, please!" Morwenna broke in quickly, aware of the turn the conversation was taking. "You're not free, Matthew! Neither of us is free to say what we feel.

I'm bound to my father's memory, just as you are bound to your mother's well-being—"

"I have to tell you Morwenna!" Gripping her arms, Matthew spoke compellingly. "I have to make you understand how I feel, why I have to bring Stefan out into the open. I can't live this life with April any more, not now I've found you again . . ."

"No!" Breaking free from his grasp, Morwenna eyed him desperately. "It's out of the question. Can't you see what we'd be doing—taking our happiness at the price of other people's?"

"*Our* happiness?" Grabbing her arm again, Matthew forced her to look at him. "So you feel the same way? If it weren't for April—if I were free . . ." His voice trailed away.

Morwenna looked away but not before he had seen his answer in her eyes. No longer could she conceal the fact, either from herself or Matthew, that the flicker of love she had felt so long ago had kindled into flame the day she had met him again; the day he had fulfilled his promise to return to Inveree. If only things had been different, she thought now. It could have been so good. But never could she have put her own happiness before that of a frail old man whose only crime had been to flee a harsh life to go in search of the only family he had left in the world. Yet, she could see by Matthew's expression that he was no longer prepared to make the same sacrifice unless—she drew a deep breath—unless she made him understand that it would be in vain.

"If you think your uncle will be allowed to stay, you're kidding yourself!" she said now. "And if you're determined to go ahead with your plans to expose him because of me, I have to make it clear to you, Matthew, that it will be wasted. I could never do that to my father's memory—or your mother and uncle." She looked at him compellingly, trying to make him understand. "You think it would free you, but you're wrong. Neither of us would ever be free—and in time we'd grow to hate each other."

"Morwenna!" Matthew tried to take her hand but she pulled away from him.

"Please—I'm tired . . ." she said

unsteadily. "It's been a long day. Couldn't we go now?"

Matthew stared at her for a moment, then let go of her arm abruptly. Leaning forward, he started the car.

Some time later, they pulled up outside the Beachcomber, Matthew watching silently as Morwenna left the car and hurried towards the guest house. Seconds later, she heard the sound of his car driving away.

Everything seemed quiet as she let herself into the house. There was no sign of Aunt Jessie and the place seemed curiously empty without the usual bustle of evening activity. Making her way to the kitchen, Morwenna poked a hesitant face round the door, only to find it empty.

"Hello."

Hearing a voice, she turned to see April Corrigan regarding her from the doorway of the dining room. Her face was slightly flushed, and, eyeing the glass the other woman was holding, Morwenna realised that she had drunk more than was good for her.

"Phil needed a part for my car; it wouldn't start," April informed her. "He took your aunt with him for company. He felt it would do her good, particularly as you weren't around to comfort her."

There was barbed criticism in her voice which Morwenna, already shaken by the revelations Matthew had made, was not prepared to tolerate.

"Where I go is my business," she said coldly, unable to conceal her loathing for the other woman any longer. "And whilst we're here, I'd like to make it plain to you, Mrs. Corrigan, that your presence here is unwelcome. Both my aunt and I have decided to close early for the winter and I'd be obliged if you'd leave as soon as possible."

"Oh dear." April made a face. "Just when I was settling down, too." She looked thoughtfully at Morwenna. "Shouldn't you consult Phil before throwing me out?"

"I run the Beachcomber!" Morwenna retorted.

"Oh, well." April gave an exaggerated sigh. "In that case, it seems I must go back to the cottage. May I stay until morning or would you prefer I left now?"

Morwenna's temper rose. "As far as I'm

concerned, the sooner you go the better!" she said crisply. "Though I doubt if you'll find a welcome at the cottage, either."

April frowned at her. "What has that husband of mine been saying to make you so angry with me?" she asked.

Morwenna's head came up. "I make my own judgments—and I made mine about you long ago," she told the other woman. Anger made her reckless then. "But, since you ask, I do know the whole story about why you and Matthew are married."

"Mm." April's eyes narrowed. "It must be serious then between you two. He would never have told you about that otherwise."

"Think what you like," Morwenna said, her face flaming, "but please leave."

"I was planning to go soon anyway!" April responded. "This island has become boring, like the people who live on it." She yawned. "I think it might be a good thing if Matthew leaves, too." Her eyes glinted. "Or did you think I'd leave him here? If so, forget it."

"Why?" Morwenna eyed her in bewilderment. "You don't love him—that's obvious. Why not let him get on with his life in peace? You have everything he owns; his name, his social position, his wealth . . ."

"All the things you'd like, in fact," April taunted. "That's why I'm not leaving him here for you to get your claws into any further."

Morwenna's face whitened. For a moment she had to fight for control, force herself not to strike out at the beautiful, mocking face in front of her. Resisting the urge with a great effort, she turned towards the door, her anger abating suddenly, leaving her dispirited and weary. The scene, coming on top of the one with Matthew and the morning's funeral, was too much for her. Tears pricked her eyelids. She hurried towards the stairs, determined that April would not see her distress. The other woman's voice floated up to her as she made her way upstairs.

"Matthew will be leaving, I can promise you that. I hope you've said your goodbyes."

Without answering, Morwenna continued upstairs, tears rolling unheeded down her face now. Reaching her father's bedroom door, she faltered, then walked quickly by, eager to reach the sanctuary of her own room.

Some time later, she heard the sound of Phil's and Aunt Jessie's voices, and made an effort to compose herself, before going downstairs to join them. Phil met her on the stairs, his face anxious.

"Where's April?" he asked, before she had a chance to speak.

Taken by surprise, she didn't reply for a moment.

"Well?" Phil's eyes searched her face.

"She's probably on her way to Smugglers' Cottage," she told him as calmly as she could. "I decided she'd been here long enough." She eyed him determinedly. Behind him, she caught a glimpse of her aunt watching from the hallway, a flicker of approval in her eyes. Encouraged, she spoke out as Phil stared frowningly at her. "I don't want her here any longer, Phil. Nor, I think, does Aunt Jessie."

"Oh? Doesn't what I want matter?" Phil's voice was deceptively calm. Eyes glinting, he stared at her.

"We run this guest house, not you!" Morwenna eyed him defiantly. "I don't want to quarrel with you over that woman, but I won't have her here any longer."

"What's Corrigan been saying, to make you talk like this?" Phil asked grimly. "And just where have you two been tonight?"

"Matthew told me nothing but the truth," Morwenna informed him. "As for where we've been, that's my business. But I will tell you this; I know a little more about April Corrigan than you do."

"Lies from Matthew Corrigan?" Phil broke in jeeringly. "He'll say anything to split us up."

"Oh, Phil!" Morwenna looked at him in irritation. "What a simpleton you are! Matthew would be delighted if April left him, I can assure you. But she won't do that; she's too fond of the things being his wife can give her."

"That's not true!" Phil said thickly.

Morwenna felt pity for him. Though she knew April was only amusing herself with him, it plainly went far deeper on his part.

"Strange—" she spoke reflectively. "Matthew told me he refused to bring April here when they were younger, because he knew she would break up our friendship. And that's exactly what she did; yours and Matthew's, mine and Matthew's—now you and I are quarrelling over her."

Phil strove to keep his feelings under control. "I don't want to quarrel with you, Morwenna—particularly on the day our father was buried." His eyes gleamed. "But I'll tell you this. I'm going to the cottage now. And I'm bringing April back with me. Do you understand?" He eyed her angrily. "I may not run the Beachcomber but I do have a financial stake in it, don't forget. And I say April stays here as long as she likes."

Without another word, Morwenna turned and walked away, towards the dining room. Moments later, she heard the door of the guest house slam and guessed Phil was carrying out his intention of bringing April back from Smugglers' Cottage.

Trembling with reaction and anger, she sank on to the nearest chair and buried her face in her hands. What had they come to, all of them? At each other's throats like a pack of hounds . . . Perhaps it would be better if Matthew did leave with April as she intended, Morwenna thought. Maybe then they could all resume their lives—as far as it was possible to do so, in the aftermath of recent events.

And, if Matthew carried out his intention of forcing his uncle to give himself up to the authorities, with all the publicity such an act would entail, there would not be peace for anyone on the island for a long time. Why couldn't Matthew have stayed in the past, along with her feelings for him—feelings which, now awakened, could only bring her anguish? For one thing was certain; April would not lightly give up what she had worked so hard to achieve.

"I've made some coffee."

Feeling her aunt's light touch on her arm, Morwenna looked up into the older woman's gently understanding eyes. Gratefully, she took the proffered cup and sipped the hot liquid.

"If Phil brings April back—" she said unsteadily, after a while, "I couldn't stay—not with her here."

"You did the right thing," Aunt Jessie murmured. "That girl was trouble for all of us."

Morwenna eyed her aunt thoughtfully, wondering if she knew more than anyone realised. She was an old woman and had seen many changes on the island over the years. Was it possible she knew about Stefan and the part Morwenna's father had played in hiding him from his pursuers?

"The fire at Smugglers' Cottage—" Morwenna eyed her aunt uncertainly. "What do you know about that, Aunt Jessie?"

The older woman eyed her back steadily. "I always felt there was more to it than just a fire caused by carelessness," she murmured. "Though when nothing further happened, I guessed I must be wrong." She eyed her niece appraisingly, but Morwenna looked away. If she was indeed unaware of what had really happened, the less she knew now, the better.

Leaning forward, the older woman smoothed back the hair from Morwenna's brow. "Why don't you think about returning to your job on the mainland?" she urged. "You ought to be with people of your own age, not buried here on the island. There's no reason for you to stay, now . . ." her voice trailed off and she looked away.

Reaching out, Morwenna touched her aunt's hand impulsively. "Not yet," she said gently, "I need time . . . we both do . . ." Making an attempt at briskness, Aunt Jessie patted her hand. "Why don't you go to bed now?" she asked. "If Phil brings that woman back, I'll handle it. I can't turn her away tonight, but I'll make it plain to both of them that I stand with you on this. She must find somewhere else to stay, first thing in the morning."

Morwenna looked at her gratefully. The last thing she wanted was to have to endure April's smugly triumphant face when she returned with Phil. She shivered instinctively. What was happening up at the cottage? Feelings would be running high. She hoped fervently that Phil and Matthew would not engage in a further clash, possibly coming to blows this time.

She made her way to her bedroom, wanting only to escape the futility of the situation they were all in; Phil hopelessly infatuated with a woman who revelled in her ability to twist him round her little finger, Matthew chaffing fruitlessly at the bonds of his enforced marriage, she herself nursing a hopeless love for him. All of them caught in a web of deceit from which they could not extricate themselves.

She fell asleep quickly, her mind exhausted by the events of the day. Sunlight was flooding into the room when she awoke the following morning, and she sat up quickly, reaching for her bedside clock, gasping as she saw the lateness of the hour. With the necessity of seeing to the guests' breakfasts removed, it seemed she and her aunt had overslept. Reaching for her dressing gown, she climbed out of bed and left her room. The door to April's room was ajar and she peered cautiously in, relieved when she realised that the woman had not, after all, returned. Nor, it seemed, had Phil. His bed, when she looked into his room, had obviously not been slept in. Frowning, she was about to return to her own room when a resounding knock on the front door attracted her attention and she realised that this was what had awakened her in the first place. Hurrying downstairs, she drew back the bolts on the heavy door and opened it, half expecting to see Phil standing there.

Instead, she found herself gazing at the burly frame of Constable Tregarth, the local policeman.

"Constable Tregarth! Is anything wrong?" Opening the door further, she stared anxiously at him.

"May I come in?" he asked.

Stepping back to allow him to enter, Morwenna waited apprehensively for him to state the purpose of his visit. Out of the corner of her eye, she saw her aunt poised on the stairs, eyeing the visitor curiously.

"You have a Mrs. Corrigan staying here, I believe?" Despite the fact that he had known Morwenna since childhood, the policeman's tone was formal.

"That's right." Licking suddenly dry lips, Morwenna eyed him uncertainly. "Is anything wrong with her?"

"There's been an accident down by the local beauty spot; that place known as Lovers' Point!" the man informed her. "A body has been found there which we believe to be that of Mrs. April Corrigan."

Waves of shock washed over Morwenna as she realised that he was telling her April was dead.

7

"I'VE made some coffee. You'll have a cup, Constable?"

To Morwenna's ears, Aunt Jessie's voice was the only normal part of the events of the last few minutes. One look at Morwenna's stricken face and the older woman had taken charge immediately. Coming down into the hallway, she had taken her niece by the arm and guided her towards the lounge. Feeling suddenly as if her legs would give way, Morwenna had been glad to sink on to the nearest chair. Now, though the first waves of shock had passed, she was still hardly able to believe that April Corrigan was dead. Accepting a cup of coffee from Aunt Jessie, the policeman took a sip, glancing in Morwenna's direction.

"I can understand it being a great shock to you," he observed. "She was a guest here, after all."

"Yes. That is—" As the man's eyebrows rose in enquiry, she hastened to explain.

"She was about to return to Smugglers' Cottage. In fact, I thought that was where she had gone last night."

Constable Tregarth wrote something down in his notebook, as she watched.

"How did it happen?" she forced herself to say.

"Her body was found at the bottom of the cliff," he told her. "Smugglers' Cottage—" Eyeing her thoughtfully, he tapped the pencil he held on his hand. "Isn't that the place her husband owns?"

"Yes." Morwenna looked across at her aunt for reassurance. "The cottage has been in the Corrigan famiy for years. Matthew—April's husband—was modernising it. It hadn't been used for a while."

"I see." The policeman looked pensive. "There was a fire there some years ago, as I recall."

At his words Morwenna tensed, her mind going back over the story Matthew's uncle had told them the previous day. She closed her eyes for a moment, still recoiling from the shock of hearing of April's death. Events seemed to be crowding in on her thick and fast, leaving her bewildered and apprehensive. As the shock began to subside a little, her mind cleared, one thought dominating it above all else. April had died at the spot where, long ago, another woman had been murdered by her husband when he discovered her infidelity. It was ridiculous, she knew; a case of her heightened emotions playing tricks on her. Yet, living on the island for most of her life, she had gradually absorbed its superstitions and, try as she might now, she could not dissociate the morning's events from the legend which surrounded the spot known as Lovers' Point. It was nonsense, she told herself angrily now. History did not repeat itself in this way; she was allowing her shocked mind to become fanciful. Yet, out of her consciousness, Matthew's words returned to her.

> "So long as April lives, the threat hangs over us and my mother can never know that her brother has been in this country for years. I can't divorce April, and I doubt if she will ever leave me."

Now, in the face of April's accident, the words had an ominous ring, filling her with fear for Matthew. She recalled April's intention of forcing him to leave the island with her, her confident assertion that he would do whatever she told him. There was bound to have been a clash of some kind when April arrived at the cottage. Taunted by a woman he despised, a woman who had a hold over him that he was powerless to break, had Matthew lost control for a moment and attacked her? A convulsive shudder went through Morwenna at the thought. It couldn't be that! There had to be some other explanation.

Constable Tregarth was eyeing her in concern and, aware of it, she made an effort to control herself. Whatever she said, whatever she did now, Matthew's fate might be in her hands. "Her husband—does he know?" she asked shakily.

The policeman shook his head. "So far we haven't been able to contact him." His voice was carefully noncommittal. "The cottage door is unlocked and there are signs that someone was living there—but we've seen nothing whatsoever of Mr. Corrigan." He eyed Morwenna shrewdly. "He was a friend, I understand?"

"Yes. Of all of us," Morwenna told him

hesitantly. "We knew him well years ago, when he used to spend the summers here with his parents."

"And you've no idea where we might find him?" the policeman pursued.

She shook her head helplessly.

"I saw him early yesterday evening, but I don't know where he went when he left me," she confessed. "Presumably back to the cottage." Turning, she looked at her aunt, seated across from her. Catching her glance, the older woman gave Morwenna's arm an encouraging pat.

"Drink your coffee," she said softly.

Obeying, Morwenna felt herself relaxing slightly as the hot liquid slid down her throat, steadying her nerves and helping her to compose herself.

"I can hardly believe it," she whispered at last.

"Aye. Well, those cliffs are treacherous in the dark, if you don't know them," the policeman asserted.

Morwenna shuddered, a mental picture filling her mind of April's body lying broken and twisted on the rocks at the bottom of the cliffs.

"It's too awful to think about," she whispered.

Her anguished mind refused to accept what had happened and the implications of Matthew's inexplicable absence. Where was he? And where was Phil? What had happened last night between the three of them? Constable Tregarth was speaking now in a kindly voice, obviously aware of her distress.

"So the last time you saw the deceased was . . ."

"About nine o'clock," Morwenna replied in a shaky voice. "She—we—felt it was time she returned to the cottage. After my father's death, Aunt Jessie and I had more or less decided to close the guest house for what was left of the season."

"Yes. Please accept my condolences on the death of your father. He was a well respected man around these parts." The policeman cleared his throat. "And your brother—I understand he's been here on holiday?" The question, innocent enough, still evoked fear in Morwenna's mind. Why hadn't Phil returned last night, bringing April with him as he had declared his intention of doing? What had happened? The unanswered questions tormented her.

"Phil is very much a nomad when he's on the island." Aunt Jessie entered the conversation, as Morwenna sought for words to answer the policeman. "He has a boat and is apt to wander off for a day or two's sailing whenever he takes it into his head to do so. He was saying to me only last night that he thought he'd take the boat out early this morning. Morwenna and I both retired early; it had been an exhausting day with the funeral and everything. Phil had gone out, as he often did, and we usually left him to see to himself when he came home late. I fell asleep quickly and so didn't hear him return. Did you, Morwenna?" Behind her spectacles, her eyes glinted in her niece's direction.

Morwenna shook her head in bewilderment. It sounded as if Aunt Jessie were trying to protect Phil, she thought in sudden horror. Surely she couldn't think . . . Her mind blanching, Morwenna turned her head away quickly from the policeman's searching gaze. Matthew's return to Inveree had plunged them all into a spiral of events which grew more confusing and frightening with each day that passed.

"I expect she was wandering about the cliffs and lost her footing," Aunt Jessie murmured, eyeing the policeman.

"Aye. I expect that's what it is." Putting away his notebook, he rose to his feet, glancing across at Morwenna. "And you've no idea where your brother is now?" he asked.

She shook her head dumbly.

"I'd like to speak to him as soon as he turns up." The policeman's tone was brisk. "And of course, we'll have a better idea of what happened when the results of the autopsy are through—and when her husband is traced," he added quietly.

For a moment Morwenna was unable to hide her thoughts. "You can't think that Matthew—"

"I don't think anything yet. I'm just making preliminary enquiries into a death," Constable Tregarth responded. "I expect someone else from our department will want to speak to you again later. In the meantime—" He looked in Aunt Jessie's direction. "I'll let myself out, Jessie. No doubt it's all been a shock and you'll need some time to reflect. If there's anything further you recall which might be of assistance, you know where to find me."

Morwenna was hardly aware of him taking his leave. Her head had begun to ache abominably; a reaction, she guessed, to the events of the last few minutes. After a sharp glance at her, Aunt Jessie saw the policeman to the door, then returned, closing the door quietly behind her.

"Well." Her voice was pensive. "This is a shock, Morwenna."

Fearfully, Morwenna eyed her. "It gets worse, doesn't it?" she murmured unsteadily. "April dead. Matthew nowhere to be found—and Phil missing, too." She swallowed. "What does it mean, Aunt Jessie?" She looked up at the older woman, who came to stand beside her quickly, taking her hand.

"I wish I knew," she murmured. She shook her head.

"Where's Phil? Why didn't he come back last night? Something must have happened at the cottage between the three of them!"

Unable to reply for a moment, Morwenna clung to the older woman's hand. Thank heavens for Aunt Jessie, she thought wretchedly. In a changing, frightening world in which she was finding out rapidly that people were not what they seemed, Aunt Jessie was the one constant factor.

"You think Phil had something to do with April's death, don't you?" she asked shakily at last. Her voice, to her own ears, sounded high and cracked.

"I don't think anything." Aunt Jessie's voice was calmly practical. "Like John Tregarth, I'm waiting on events. And until either Matthew or Phil turns up, there's little else we can do, I'm afraid."

"Where are they?" Morwenna spoke with sudden anguish. "Why have they both disappeared like this?" Her voice rose. "Maybe they're dead, too. Maybe something dreadful happened out there—"

"Don't be silly!" Aunt Jessie's voice was sharply commanding. "I'm convinced there's some simple explanation to all this."

"Simple?" Morwenna looked at her wildly. "Nothing has been simple since Matthew came back here! And they *could* be dead—remember the legend?" Her voice quivered. "The fight between the husband and the lover; the lover killed and the husband hanged for murder—"

"Stop it, Morwenna!" Aunt Jessie shook her niece's arm slightly. "You're overwrought and letting your imagination run away with you! That legend is just a story handed down from one generation to another, part of the island's folklore. This is real. Now try and pull yourself together. Phil, when he returns, and Matthew too, when he's found, are going to need all the help they can get."

Sitting down, the older woman gathered Morwenna into her arms. "All we can do is wait and try to keep calm."

Morwenna clung to her for a moment, making a determined effort to pull herself together. At last, she calmed a little.

"Why did you and April quarrel last night?" Aunt Jessie asked suddenly. Morwenna hesitated. Then, at last, the story began to come out, haltingly at first, then with a torrent of words as she unburdened herself.

"So that's it." Aunt Jessie murmured, when she had finished. "I guessed there was something odd going on at the time of the fire. I hinted as much to you last night." She looked thoughtfully into space for some moments. "We mustn't let the police know about this if we can help it," she said then, rousing herself. "It will provide them with the perfect motive for Matthew, if they're looking for one."

"But they can't believe he did it!" Morwenna protested. "It has to have been an accident! He isn't capable of murder."

"Anyone's capable of murder, given enough provocation!" Aunt Jessie pointed out.

Morwenna frowned, trying to recall the conversation she'd had with April the previous evening. "She was already slightly drunk before she left here," she remembered. "She could easily have lost her balance along the cliff path—"

"In that case, why didn't Phil return?" Aunt Jessie queried. "If he hadn't found her, he would surely have come back, thinking she might have made her way back here."

"Do you really think he's gone out sailing?" Morwenna eyed her aunt shrewdly. The older woman clasped her hands together, shaking her head.

"He did mention it, on the way back from the garage—and I had to tell John Tregarth something; play for time," she answered. "If he'd known Phil didn't return last night after following April to the cottage, there would have been no doubt in his mind that Phil was connected in some way with April's death. And we don't know for sure that he didn't come back, then left again early today." But her voice lacked conviction. "I just hope we don't get into trouble for not telling John Tregarth Phil had gone to the cottage after April."

"They think Matthew killed her, anyway!" Morwenna insisted. "I know they do."

"You love him, don't you?" Aunt Jessie eyed her shrewdly.

Morwenna looked away from the older woman's penetrating gaze.

"I think I always have," she admitted at last. "I must have known in some way that he'd return to the island one day and I wanted to be here when he did. Looking after Dad was only part of the reason for my return, I can see that now." Her voice trembled. "I don't think I could bear it if they found he killed April," she added quietly.

Aunt Jessie's eyes glinted behind her spectacles. "You might have to face the fact that he did," she murmured. "He had enough cause to hate her and want to be rid of her, from what you've told me."

Morwenna felt a chill go through her at her aunt's words, recognising the truth of them.

The morning passed slowly in an agony of suspense, both women moving quietly about, trying to keep their minds occupied, yet with ears strained for the sound of the door bell. At last, Morwenna slipped outside for a walk, unable to bear the strain of waiting any longer. Hands in anorak pockets, she wandered along the road leading to the village, thankful for the breeze which fanned her cheeks. The questions which had tormented her all morning receded somewhat in the normality of every day life in the village. Everything seemed quiet; people going about their work as usual. Only at the cottage had time seemed to stand still. She slowed, watching for a moment before turning towards the beach, catching sight as she did so, of Constable Tregarth walking along some yards ahead of her. Increasing her pace, she drew level with him.

"Hello!" She caught at his arm as he turned in the direction of the police station further along the road. "Have you, that is —is there anything new . . . ?"

"Morwenna!" His weathered face creased in a smile and he touched her arm lightly. "Out for a breath of air? Good!"

She nodded, concealing her impatience as best she could. Walking along beside her, the policeman said nothing further for a few moments.

"We've located Mr. Corrigan," he told her then. "He was at his home on the mainland. One or two of the fishermen we questioned this morning remembered him looking for someone to take him across yesterday evening. Apparently he was in a hurry to leave the island. The man who did agree to take him told us he'd put him ashore in the late evening, from where he made his way to a taxi rank. In too much of a hurry, evidently, to wait for the ferry this morning, when he could have taken his own car with him. They're questioning him now over on the mainland." He glanced enquiringly at her. "The plain-clothes boys not been to see you yet?"

Morwenna shook her head, not trusting herself to answer. Fear had overwhelmed her at his words and the colour had drained from her face.

"They don't think—they can't think . . ." she looked at the policeman entreatingly.

"Why not wait and see?" Tregarth's voice was gently reassuring. "The truth will come out soon enough. And now I'll be saying cheerio." About to leave her, he turned as if struck by a sudden thought. "No sign of your brother yet then?" he enquired, eyeing her keenly.

"Not yet. I'm sure he'll be back any time, though." Morwenna strove to keep some semblance of normality in her voice. As the policeman left her with a cheery nod, she walked on, her mind in turmoil. Why had Matthew been trying to leave the island in such a hurry last night? And where—*where* was Phil? Despite her horror at April's death, anger burned suddenly in Morwenna. She had brought chaos to all of them in her ruthless pursuit of her own ends.

Increasing her step, she hurried back to the Beachcomber, hardly pausing to close the door behind her as she entered. Aunt Jessie came towards her immediately, and the sight of her had a calming effect on Morwenna.

"They've found Matthew!" she said quickly. "He left the island last night; one of the fishermen rowed him over—"

"Where was he when they found him?" Aunt Jessie asked.

Putting a steadying hand up to her face, Morwenna fought for control. "At his home," she said at last.

"Well, then . . ." Aunt Jessie's voice was briskly reassuring. "That isn't the action of a guilty man, is it—sitting at home waiting for the police to come for him?"

"But leaving the island like that—not even waiting for the ferry . . ." Morwenna looked at the older woman helplessly.

"He will have his reasons," Aunt Jessie interrupted firmly. "And they'll all come out in the end. Now how about some lunch?"

"Still no sign of Phil, I suppose?" Morwenna looked at her aunt anxiously as she followed her towards the kitchen.

"Not yet, but I'm sure he won't be long." The flicker of anxiety in the older woman's eyes belied her reassuring words.

The two women ate in silence, each preoccupied with her own thoughts. Despite the appetising meal Aunt Jessie had prepared, Morwenna picked at it, her mind filled with apprehension. What was Matthew telling them at the police station? Was he, even now, confessing to the murder of his wife? Her mind recoiled from the thought. She could not believe Matthew was capable of such a thing, whatever the provocation. There had to be some rational explanation for it all, yet how could she—how could Matthew—explain why he had decided to leave the island so suddenly? He had not mentioned any plans to leave when she had visited St. Anselm's with him the previous evening. Surely he would have done so? No matter how she tried to analyse the situation, Morwenna's mind kept returning to that one indisputable fact: Matthew had more than sufficient motive for killing April—

and his action in leaving the island so precipitately did nothing to lessen any suspicions the police might have. She put a hand to her head, aware that it was still aching abominably. She had not slept well the previous evening, and the morning's events had not improved matters. Anxiety crippled her ability to think straight, forcing her to wander about restlessly, unable to settle to anything for long. As time passed, with no sign of Phil and no further news of Matthew, her nerves stretched. Her mind, up till now closed to the admission of anything but Matthew's innocence, was opening, chink by chink, to the hitherto unimaginable . . .

"Why don't you try to have a nap?" Aunt Jessie was eyeing her critically from across the table. "You look shattered."

"I doubt if I could sleep," Morwenna shrugged.

"Try!" Aunt Jessie urged. Standing up, she pushed back her chair. "I think I'll pop to the supermarket—a walk might do me good." Her eyes softened as she looked at Morwenna. "I'll try to have a word with John Tregarth, too; see what I can find out about Matthew." Her eyes gleamed for a moment. "I've known John since he was a boy; if anyone can get anything out of him, it's me."

Smiling wryly in spite of herself, Morwenna followed her aunt out of the kitchen into the lounge, curling herself up in the armchair by the big window. Her eyes closed . . . Half asleep, she roused herself some minutes later, at the sound of her aunt's voice. Turning, she saw that lady watching her, eyes twinkling, from the door.

"I thought you wouldn't be able to sleep," she murmured.

Smiling drowsily, Morwenna raised a hand in farewell. She hardly heard the older woman leave the house.

It seemed like only moments later that she felt her arm being shaken and was jerked into wakefulness, to find her brother Phil standing by the chair.

"Phil!"

Instantly sleep left her and she jumped to her feet, almost laughing in her relief. Unshaven, obviously still in yesterday's clothes, Phil looked haggard, and her relief quickly turned into concern.

"Where have you been—they're looking for you . . ."

"I've been out in the boat. Sorry I didn't let you know." His reply was abrupt. Moving restlessly round the room, he was obviously disturbed and Morwenna watched him in mounting apprehension. He swung round suddenly to face her.

"I had to get out on the water; you know how I am when things have gone badly . . ." He stopped, frowning. "What do you mean—they're looking for me? You haven't reported me missing or anything like that?" His eyes flickered with annoyance. "I'm not a kid, you know."

Eyeing him, Morwenna was temporarily lost for words. "Don't you know . . ." she asked hesitantly at last.

"Know what? What's the matter?" Quick alarm flickered in Phil's eyes. "There's nothing wrong—Aunt Jessie . . ."

"It's not Aunt Jessie—it's April." Morwenna's voice wobbled dangerously. "I thought you might have heard—she's dead, Phil . . ."

Phil's face whitened and he took a step

backwards, putting out a hand as if warding off some unseen menace. "Dead? April?" He spoke with difficulty, after a moment. "She can't be . . ." His voice trailing off, he looked uncomprehendingly at Morwenna.

Watching him, Morwenna was conscious of a flood of relief. Knowing him as she did, she was certain he was not putting on an act for her benefit. He really didn't know about April's death . . .

Breathing jerkily, he crossed to the window and leaned against it, his body sagging. "I don't believe it," he muttered at last.

Moving to his side, Morwenna touched his arm. "I'm sorry, Phil." Her voice was unsteady. "I know how you felt about her."

For a few moments there was silence between them.

"How—what happened?" Phil asked at last.

"She was found at the bottom of the cliff early this morning, near the waterfall," Morwenna told him. "They don't know if she fell or . . ." Her voice broke suddenly. Overcome by the emotion she had been holding back all morning, she buried her head against her brother's shoulder and wept. "Oh, Phil!" Her voice, muffled against him, was anguished. "They think Matthew . . . They have him at the police station."

Instantly Phil put his arms round her, saying nothing until her sobs subsided slightly.

"But why would they think Matthew . . ." His tone was puzzled when he spoke at last.

"He wanted to get away from her; she'd tricked him into marrying her . . ." Morwenna's words tumbled over themselves. "Oh, Phil—it was because of me! I knew last night he loved me—that if it weren't for April . . ."

"Whatever he said to you last night, he didn't kill April!" Phil said flatly. "She was alive when he left for the mainland. She told me herself that's where he'd gone; apart from that, I saw him on the jetty myself about to climb aboard a fisherman's boat, as I made my way to Smugglers' Cottage. I remember wishing savagely that he'd stay away and never come back, as I stood watching him."

Hope had dawned in Morwenna's eyes and she clutched her brother's jacket convulsively. "You saw him leaving?" She hardly dared believe it.

Phil nodded.

"April was alone at the cottage when I arrived. She told me Matthew had decided to return to the mainland; I wasn't clear exactly why he'd decided to go, but they'd obviously had words. He must have made up his mind in a hurry because he left his car—"

"Oh, Phil!" Morwenna's eyes shone. "This means you can clear him—" She broke off, noting the look of anguished horror which had crossed her brother's face.

"She must have decided to go alone," he murmured then, half to himself.

"What?" Morwenna eyed him apprehensively.

"I was all for her coming back here to the Beachcomber with me." Pausing, Phil was obviously finding it difficult to continue. "I said I was glad Matthew had gone because I was sick of this hole in the corner business. I wanted us to be open about our relationship; no more sneaking round behind Matthew's back. I—I told her it was about time she left him for good, particularly as he knew the way things were between us." His fingers, gripping the window sill, showed white under the sudden pressure of his hands. Biting his lip, he averted his face from his sister's gaze. "She laughed at me, Morwenna!" he said harshly at last. "Told me I was crazy if I thought she was going to leave Matthew for—" his voice choked—"for a *fisherman's* son!" His voice, raw with pain, faltered momentarily, before he managed to control it. "She told me she was happy with things the way they were —and if I didn't like it, I could forget the whole thing. There were other men . . ." He was silent for a moment. "You were right, Wenny!" His voice thickened then, a savage note entering it. "She had been using me, playing me and Matthew off against each other. Laughing at us both, all the while!" Turning, he stared into his sister's horror filled face. "But I didn't kill her, Wenny—you have to believe that!"

When she didn't reply, continuing to stare at him with anguished eyes, he grabbed her arm, shaking it roughly.

"Do you hear me?" He was shouting now in his anxiety. "I didn't kill her! Though I felt as if I'd like to kill her, at that moment!" His voice quietened. "She obviously expected me to play along, accept the terms she had laid down. She suggested going for a moonlight swim; we'd done that before several times, taking the hidden path down to the beach; the one the smugglers always used." Contempt entered his voice. "She even tried to sweet talk me back into a good mood again, obviously wanting things to stay as they were between us. I pushed her away . . . I was filled with disgust—for her and for myself. She'd been playing me for a sucker all along. Anyway—" His voice hardened. "I refused; told her to go to hell, in fact! I left the cottage then and wandered around for a while. I felt sick, Wenny—the last thing I wanted to do was come back here to face you and Aunt Jessie just then, knowing you expected me to bring April back with me. So I ended up doing what I always do—always have done since I was a boy, when things got me down. I headed for my boat and put out to sea. I sailed around for a while, then put into a little cove further along the coast when it became too rough to stay on the water. I still didn't feel like coming home and I must have fallen asleep. When I woke up, it was morning. I still felt pretty rough, so I sailed around again for a while before making my way back here." Finishing, he walked across to a chair and slumped into it, putting his head in his hands.

"She must have decided to go swimming on her own—" his voice was muffled. "And, being half drunk . . ." he left the sentence unfinished.

Morwenna had been listening intently and it was a few moments before she spoke. "It's too horrible for words," she said at last.

She had a mental picture of April, tottering drunkenly about on the cliff path. Shuddering, she turned away.

"You believe me, don't you Wenny?" Phil was looking entreatingly at her now. "I—I wouldn't have harmed her . . ."

"Yes, of course!"

Crossing to him, she put an arm round his shoulders, realising again how great a shock the news of April's death must have been to him.

"I think I always knew what she was like, deep down!" he muttered eventually, "But I just closed my eyes to it. She was so beautiful, Wenny—" His voice broke off.

Morwenna's arm tightened round his shoulder. "Yes, she was beautiful," she agreed quietly. "Phil—" she looked at him urgently for a moment. "You said you saw Matthew leaving for the mainland. That means you can clear him. The police are questioning him now."

Phil moved restlessly. "I need time to think," he muttered.

Morwenna stared at him in alarm. "There's nothing to think about, Phil!" she protested. "They want to speak to you anyway."

"Do the police know I went to the cottage looking for April last night?" Phil asked.

"No—I . . ." Breaking off, Morwenna stared at him aghast. "You can't be contemplating keeping quiet?" She clutched his arm, a wild note creeping into her voice "For heaven's sake, Phil—don't even think it! You can get Matthew out of this—"

"And who's going to get *me* out of this?" he broke in harshly. Turning, he stared at her. "Tell me—who, Wenny? I had just as much of a motive as he did and I can't prove April was alive when I left her."

"Phil!" Crouching down beside his chair, Morwenna looked compellingly at him. "You must tell them everything! It will all come out anyway and then they'll know you concealed information. How will they believe anything you say, after that?"

"But they'll think I did it!" Phil's eyes were filled with horror. "I have no witness, no one to corroborate my story. They'll charge me with murder!"

"They haven't said anything about murder!" Morwenna argued desperately. "It was a tragic accident. She was drunk; I knew that, even before she left here."

"You think they'll believe that, once they know I was at the cottage?" Phil's voice was bitter. "You're my sister; they'd expect you to back up what I said."

"They have to believe it!" she said. "You have to go to them and tell them the truth, Phil, for your own sake as well as for Matthew's. Don't you see that?"

"I see that I'm going to be left taking the blame for something I didn't do, whilst the rich man's son gets away—as always!" he said bitterly.

"That's not true! Face it, Phil—you and Matthew had no quarrel until April came between you. And there's something you don't know about April—" Her voice trembled and Phil looked at her quickly.

"What don't I know?" he demanded.

Morwenna hesitated for only a second, then she told him the whole story of Stefan's defection and subsequent escape to St. Anselm's. When she reached the part where April had blackmailed Matthew into marriage, she saw Phil's eyes fill with horror. Reaching out, she took his hand, feeling his fingers tightening in hers. He didn't speak for a while after she had finished the story.

"I never realised she was so—bad," he whispered then. After a while, he straightened up, making a determined effort to compose himself.

"Matthew kept quiet because of his

father—and ours," Morwenna murmured then. "They're both dead now; they can't be hurt. But Matthew needs your help, Phil. You're the only one who *can* help him."

"I've no choice, have I?" Phil's voice was heavy with resignation. Standing up, he looked into his sister's eyes. "The sooner I go, the better."

"Let me come with you!" Morwenna was beginning, before he interrupted. "You stay here and look after Aunt Jessie. If they don't believe my version of events, you two are going to need each other. And the less said about what happened years ago, the better. We may be able to keep that part to ourselves; no reason why the old man should suffer unnecessarily." Turning, he walked towards the door. Morwenna followed him, her eyes filled with anxiety.

"They'll believe you," She caught at Phil's arm as he opened the front door. "And Matthew will do everything he can to help you."

"Why should he?" Phil's mouth twisted. "After the way April and I made such a fool of him, why should he?"

Turning, he stepped through the doorway and when Morwenna reached it, it was to see his tall figure striding down the street with a determined step.

8

THE sea looked calm and inviting under the late afternoon sun. Despite its warmth, Morwenna shivered slightly, drawing her anorak closer about her. She had wandered round the beach for hours, unable to bear the confines of the house after Phil had left. Not even waiting for Aunt Jessie's return, she had obeyed an impulse, grabbing her outdoor things and leaving the house. Now, seated on one of the large boulders which littered the area, she could not prevent her eyes from straying, as they had done several times already, to the cliffs further down the coastline where the waterfall cascaded down into a clearing before dropping sharply away to the beach below. *Lovers' Point*. A dangerous place, yet with such a romantic name. A place around which a legend had woven itself; a legend which, despite being rooted in the past, seemed now to have become curiously merged with the present.

It was late, she knew. Yet she had no wish to return to the Beachcomber. Here she could pretend time stood still and that yesterday's tragedy had not happened. Here, too, she could hold back the future consequences of that tragedy until she was ready to face them.

"Mowenna?"

She had not heard his quiet approach and when she turned in answer, it was to see Matthew watching her from a few yards away.

"I just came in on one of the fishing boats," he said, watching her closely. "The police let me go without any reason."

"Phil told them April was alive when you left for the mainland." The wind tossed Morwenna's words back to her.

Approaching cautiously, Matthew nodded. "I thought something like that must have happened," he said.

"So now you're free." Morwenna tried to smile up at him, then her face crumpled suddenly.

Matthew was by her side in a moment, his arms round her, holding her tightly whilst she struggled to control her tears.

Instinctively she knew that if there was a way of proving Phil innocent, should it become necessary, Matthew would find it.

"Tell me what happened," he said at last, when her tears had spent themselves.

Seating her back on the boulder, he perched beside her, listening as she explained the part Phil had played in the previous evening's events, holding her close without interrupting until she had finished.

"So April wanted to go swimming." His voice was thoughtful then. "They told me she was wearing a swimsuit when she was found, and there were several broken pieces of glass—probably from a bottle—not far away from her body. That ties in with Phil's story, and should help him."

Held close in his arms, Morwenna gave up trying to think. The events of the last few hours had been going round and round in circles in her mind. Now, totally exhausted, she was content to let Matthew take over.

"If only there was a witness . . ." Matthew hesitated, brow furrowed, then spoke again, his voice suddenly urgent.

"Come on, Morwenna!"

Pulling her to her feet, he took her hand and hurried her across the beach. Morwenna eyed him expectantly as he headed for the harbour, crossing it in rapid strides and leaving at the other side. Crunching on to the jetty, he walked determinedly towards a group of fishermen, busy with their nets. Several eyed them with interest as they drew near; yet, ignoring them, Matthew drew Morwenna to where a lone fisherman worked some yards further down the beach. Morwenna recognised the man as Wyn Roberts, her father's erstwhile shipmate. Blue eyes eyed their approach warily from beneath shaggy eyebrows and he turned his back on them as they drew near.

"It's me again." Matthew's tone was determined.

The man nodded curtly. "I can't take you to the mainland: I told you that last night and I'm telling you again." His voice was surly as he addressed Matthew.

"So you did," Matthew responded. Turning, he indicated Morwenna. "You know Morwenna, I think."

"Aye." Wyn nodded in her direction.

"Hello, Wyn." She greeted him readily, holding out her hand which he took without hesitation, though she noticed he gave Matthew a wide berth.

"You obviously remember then my coming to ask you if you could take me to the mainland." Matthew eyed the older man speculatively.

"I had no time!" Wyn's voice was sharp.

Matthew made a placatory gesture. "It's okay. But I'd be interested to know, Wyn—how long did you stay down here on the beach?"

Wyn eyed him watchfully. "What's it to you?" he asked.

Matthew ran a distracted hand through his hair, eyeing the other man appealingly. "Look, I know you don't like the Corrigans—"

"You've no right to come here spoiling the place." Wyn scowled in Matthew's direction. "We don't want holiday cottages on Inveree—and we don't want the likes of you."

Morwenna understood then. She had been mystified by Wyn's apparent hostility towards Matthew, particularly as he'd been one of Ralph Corrigan's staunchest friends on the island.

"There's to be no holiday complex, Wyn!" she said quickly now. "That was just a rumour, probably started by my brother, without any proof. Matthew never had any intention of undertaking such a project, as we now know."

The old man eyed her appraisingly for a moment. "Should think not," he muttered then, turning away.

"Anyway, now that's settled—" Matthew spoke again in a determined voice. "The fact is, Wyn, there was an accident last night up by Lovers' Point, on the old path which the smugglers used, leading up to my cottage." Turning, he pointed in the direction of the cliffs. "Did you, by any chance, hear about it?"

"No. Been at sea all day." Wyn's voice had lost some of its curtness. Matthew eyed him thoughtfully. "It's possible then you being here last night, you saw someone—my wife—" his voice shook slightly, "on that path last night. She fell, you see. What I'm driving at, Wyn, is would you have seen her at all on the cliff path and if so, was there anyone else with her or was she alone? Could you help us out, do you think?"

The man treated him to a long stare. "And if I did see her?" he asked gruffly, after a moment.

"If you did," Matthew said slowly, "you had better say so. Because they are holding Morwenna's brother down at the police station. He saw my wife last night, and she was alive when he left her yet there's no way he can prove he wasn't with her when she fell from the path. Unless, of course, someone saw her."

Wyn shifted his feet, poking at the ground, whilst Morwenna watched, her eyes fixed on his face. "You only have to tell the truth, Wyn!" she said unsteadily, when he didn't reply. "That's all anybody wants. The truth."

There was a short silence.

"She was up there, all right!" Wyn said at last. "Weaving about on the path—" he pointed in the direction of the cliff, his voice filled with disgust. "Drunk she was, by the look of it. Singing at the top of her voice, too. Aye—she was alone. I only saw her for a few moments, mind. I was busy with my nets, minding my own business.

When I looked again, she had gone; I assumed she'd gone back up to the cottage."

Morwenna was aware of Matthew's hand tightening in her own, the muscles working in his face.

"You didn't hear anything—a scream, perhaps?" He was watching Wyn closely now.

Wyn bent over his net. "Who's to say who it was screaming?" he asked after a moment. "No human sound, that, on dark winter nights. Who's to say this was any different?"

Hearing him, Morwenna understood. She had forgotten the islanders' belief that the place known as Lovers' Point was haunted. If it had not been for that, Wyn might have realised April had fallen. Her face shadowed. So April, who had laughed at the legend, had died because of it . . . For a moment, Morwenna's sadness was unbearable. She turned away, waiting quietly for Matthew to finish his business.

"And you'd be prepared to say that to the police?" he was asking now.

Wyn hesitated, then, with a look in

Morwenna's direction, nodded. "Thanks, Wyn. From all of us."

Morwenna's voice was husky. Turning, she ran back across the beach, past the curious gaze of the other fishermen, towards the shelter of the beach wall. By the time Matthew had reached her, she had regained control of herself. Taking her arm, he looked searchingly into her eyes.

"Are you all right?" he asked.

She nodded, not trusting herself to speak.

"You know what this means, Morwenna?" Matthew's voice was rough with emotion. "We can prove that Phil told the truth." His voice rose exultantly. "It's going to be all right, Morwenna. After all that's happened, it's going to be all right." Pulling her into his arms, he held her to him, and she felt his heart beating against hers. For a moment she was still, content just to be there, not speaking. She felt tired; relief had not come yet and she hardly dared believe, after all her fears, that it was going to be all right for Phil. As for the future—she drew in a deep, shuddering breath. The future could wait. It would be a while before she stopped picturing a slender figure tottering on the cliff path or fancied she heard a scream high on the wind.

"Why did you leave the island so suddenly?" She had to know.

Matthew's face sobered. "I'd already decided to go before April arrived at the cottage," he told her. "I had plenty of time to think, after I dropped you off at the Beachcomber. After what you'd said, it seemed to me the only way was to leave, get back to work, let things carry on as they were between April and me. You'd told me there was no hope for us, and I realised I couldn't expose Stefan in the end. How could I do to my mother what my father had not been able to bring himself to do? No matter what I said about the Government being sympathetic towards Stefan, I knew I couldn't take the risk." His voice was suddenly husky. "So when April arrived, half drunk, taunting me, I forestalled her by just packing my stuff and leaving. I couldn't stand it a minute longer, listening to her, watching her and Phil make a fool of me. But the worst part was knowing you were so near, yet out of my reach." He bent his head and she felt his breath on her cheek. "I've always loved you, Morwenna—even when you were a little girl trailing around behind Phil and me. I always will love you. But if, in the circumstances, you'd rather I went away again—"

Morwenna clutched at him convulsively. "No!" Her voice was a whisper. "Don't go . . ."

Matthew held her tightly and after a while, she felt his lips seeking hers . . .

"What about your Uncle Stefan?" Pulling away from him some time later, she stared anxiously into his face. "Will you tell the police all that happened?" Matthew shook his head. "As far as I'm concerned, my uncle died in the fire at the cottage," he told her. "The man at St. Anselm's is Brother Stephen. No one else, apart from your family and mine, knows any different, as far as I'm aware. And if it's left to me, the matter ends there. There's no reason why anyone else should know; apart from my mother, whom I'll bring to see him as soon as possible. It's all in the past, Morwenna. Stefan has suffered enough." He stared into her face. "What about you? Will you go back to the mainland and resume your career?"

Morwenna shook her head. She had not had a chance to think about that, but now her answer came without hesitation. "This is where I belong, Matthew. The only place where I could be happy."

Matthew acknowledged her decision with a nod. "Now that everything's sorted out, I have to . . ." his voice faltered. "That is, there will be arrangements to make for the funeral and taking April's body to the mainland. I'll have to leave again, once I know Phil is going to be all right."

Morwenna nodded. She had not thought anything else.

"I never expected this to happen." Matthew's voice was low. "But now it has, I can't play the part of the grieving husband. All I can do is see things are done properly . . ." His voice trailed away. Tucking his arm into Morwenna's he turned towards the village.

It was several days before Matthew was able to leave the island. He came to say goodbye, striding up the garden path to where Morwenna and her aunt waited.

Behind them, Phil hovered uneasily. For a moment, the two men stared at each other, then Matthew held out his hand. After a slight hesitation, Phil took it. Their handclasp was firm, a promise of a new beginning when the pain of the old had lessened. The past was gone and could not be changed. Phil was leaving soon, Morwenna knew. Inveree, with its memories, was too much for him at the moment. Soon, only Morwenna and Aunt Jessie would be left, yet she knew that, when the time was right, Matthew would return. He would be free then, to offer her his love, a love which, she knew now, had been hers always.

We hope this Large Print edition gives you the pleasure and enjoyment we ourselves experienced in its publication.

There are now more than 2,000 titles available in this ULVERSCROFT Large print Series. Ask to see a Selection at your nearest library.

The Publisher will be delighted to send you, free of charge, upon request a complete and up-to-date list of all titles available.

Ulverscroft Large Print Books Ltd.
The Green, Bradgate Road
Anstey
Leicestershire
LE7 7FU
England